Hate these girls? So do we.

"Did you pull it up?" Bess called from inside her never-ending closet, out of sight. "What's it say?"

"It's just how Lexi described—pretty much an online burn book," I said. "Someone is really out to destroy her."

I looked closer at the photograph, then read the caption beneath the photo:

Tired of being taken over by the self-proclaimed hottest clique in school?

Tired of missing out on the chance to date that guy you've had your eye on because you know he only has eyes for blond bombshell (slash airhead) Lexi Claremont?

Thought you had a chance at becoming Daughter of River Heights? Dream on. This girl and her carbon-copy friends rule the school, and we shouldn't have to take it anymore!

NANCY DREW

Available from Aladdin

CAROLYN KEENE

NANCY DREW

GIRL DETECTIVE®

SECRET SABOTAGE

#42

**Book One in the
Sabotage Mystery Trilogy**

Aladdin

New York   London   Toronto   Sydney

This book is a work of fiction. Any references to historical events, real people, or real locales are used fictitiously. Other names, characters, places, and incidents are the product of the author's imagination, and any resemblance to actual events or locales or persons, living or dead, is entirely coincidental.

❦ ALADDIN

An imprint of Simon & Schuster Children's Publishing Division
1230 Avenue of the Americas, New York, NY 10020
First Aladdin paperback edition June 2010
Copyright © 2010 by Simon & Schuster, Inc.
All rights reserved, including the right of reproduction in whole or
in part in any form.
ALADDIN is a trademark of Simon & Schuster, Inc., and related logo is a registered trademark of Simon & Schuster, Inc.
NANCY DREW, NANCY DREW: GIRL DETECTIVE, and related logo are registered trademarks of Simon & Schuster, Inc.
For information about special discounts for bulk purchases, please contact Simon & Schuster Special Sales at 1-866-506-1949 or business@simonandschuster.com.
The Simon & Schuster Speakers Bureau can bring authors to your live event. For more information or to book an event contact the Simon & Schuster Speakers Bureau at 1-866-248-3049 or visit our website at www.simonspeakers.com.
Designed by Sammy Yuen Jr.
The text of this book was set in Bembo.
Manufactured in the United States of America/0410 OFF
10 9 8 7 6 5 4 3 2 1
Library of Congress Control Number 2009938293
ISBN 978-1-4169-9069-7
ISBN 978-1-4424-0663-6 (eBook)

Table of Contents

THE PERFECT DRESS

"It has to be perfect," my friend Bess reiterated, twirling around in the three-sided mirror outside the dressing room. "This year is supposed to be the biggest River Heights Celebration yet!"

I glanced over at the cobalt blue sundress she wore. It complemented her shoulder-length blond hair and blazing blue eyes. "Well," I said, "if you're looking for perfect, I think you found it."

George joined us, several strange-looking gadgets clutched in her hands. "I left you guys for the antiques section an hour ago. Bess, you've probably found fifteen perfects since then!"

I stifled a laugh. Bess and George were both my

closest friends in the world, and they got along fine—but they were cousins and couldn't be more polar opposites, both in fashion sense and personality. While Bess was ultrafeminine, friendly, and took pride in having the nicest clothes (while spending the least amount of money possible on them), George was more of a tech-head and didn't care how much her hobbies cost.

Bess bit her lip and turned to the side once again, surveying the outfit. "Nancy?" she asked me.

"Perfect," I repeated.

George plopped down beside me on the bench in front of the dressing room and surveyed her cousin. "I don't get why this year is so important," she said. "There's a River Heights Celebration every year. Why would this one be any different?"

Bess cocked her hip and turned from the mirror to face me and George. "I can't believe you guys haven't heard *anything* about this one. People have been talking about it for months."

I raised an eyebrow. Usually I was pretty up on what was going on around town. But lately I'd been so busy solving mysteries, I'd obviously missed something good.

Mrs. Myrtle, an older woman who owned the vintage clothing store we were in, Boom Babies, sniffed at us and passed by with a glint of suspicion in her wrinkle-edged eyes.

I groaned inwardly, and Bess gave me an empathetic, knowing look. As an amateur detective in a town as small as River Heights, every time people saw me, they had a tendency to assume I was investigating them for some reason or another. But I couldn't blame them—oftentimes they were right.

"This year is the eightieth Celebration," Bess explained. "And Mrs. Mahoney is donating a ton of money to make it the best and most exciting Celebration yet. This is no ordinary town picnic. They're setting up an entire carnival at River Heights High—rides, fireworks, and everything."

George suddenly looked up from fussing with her pile of gadgets. "Rides?"

"Wow," I said. "That's an awful lot compared to past years. What do you think made Mrs. Mahoney decide to put so much money into it?"

Bess shrugged, just as George asked, "What kind of rides? Are we talking carousels or roller coasters?"

"I heard that there's going to be a huge roller coaster going up today—but no one will be able to ride until Friday night, when the carnival opens. And fireworks will be set off at nine o'clock, so it will be dark."

"Yes!" George exclaimed, looking at me expectantly.

"Oh, don't look at me," I warned. "I'll stick to the carousels with Bess." Sure, I enjoyed the occasional criminal investigation. But even one of my best friends in the world wouldn't be able to convince me to step foot on a roller coaster.

"So we're agreed, this is *the* dress?" Bess asked.

"Yes," I said with certainty. "But I have to admit, my judgment might have become clouded by my desperate need for caffeine. Do you guys mind if I run over and grab a caramel macchiato from Club Coffee? It's just a couple of stores away."

"Ooh, count me in!" said Bess, giving the sundress one final twirl in front of the mirror.

"I could go for a green tea," George put in.

I focused all my energy on one single image while Mrs. Myrtle rang up my friends' finds on the register: an extra-large, extra-carameled, and extra whipped-creamed caramel macchiato.

"You'd think this was the only place in all of River Heights that serves coffee," George remarked as we walked into a bustling Club Coffee.

"True," said Bess. "But there's only one Club Coffee— in River Heights, anyway. I think they've invented more coffee drinks than anyone else in the world."

I scanned the room. Every single table was filled— people were sitting alone at their laptops, others were hanging with their friends, and clusters of people dotted the room, waiting for the chance empty table. The baristas were running around at a crazy pace, making me wonder if they'd been sampling some of their own products.

I pulled my PDA from my purse and checked the time on the upper left-hand corner of the screen: 2:35 p.m.

"School must have just gotten out," I said.

"Another mystery solved." Bess giggled.

We placed our orders and stood by the pickup counter. I surveyed the room to see if anyone looked as if they were about ready to leave. My feet were aching from searching for Bess's "perfect dress" all day, and all I wanted to do was sit down and rest.

My eyes drifted over to a corner table that looked vacant, except for a small pile of papers in the center.

"Hey, you guys——," I started, but then saw that the occupant of the table had been underneath it, searching for an outlet for her laptop.

When the girl sat back up, I saw that she had midnight black hair, short and cut at a dramatic angle, with blunt-cut bangs. A single barrette, black with a plastic, sparkly red heart at the clasp, held back a small portion of her hair. She had heavy, dramatic cat's-eye eyeliner and wore all black—something I might wear prowling around, following suspects at night. It was a stark contrast against her ruby red lipstick and powder-pale skin. A bracelet adorned her wrist—a simple black string with a single ceramic red heart dangling from it.

"Nancy Drew!"

I blew out a breath, grateful to finally hear the barista call my name. But when I looked up, there was no drink on the counter.

That's when I felt a sort of sharp poke in my shoulder. I turned abruptly.

"Nancy Drew?" she asked again.

"Yes?" I said, searching the stranger's face for some hint as to how I might know her.

She had gorgeous platinum blond hair done in the kind of beachy curls that looked effortless, but you knew took a ton of time to achieve. She wore natural-looking but flawless makeup, including the perfect shade of pink, shimmery gloss—recently reapplied.

The girl thrust her hand toward me, and I reached out to shake it. She had a surprisingly strong grip for someone so slim and with such . . . pink clothes.

"I'm Lexi?" she asked. "Lexi Claremont?" I felt my face growing warm. Was I supposed to know this girl?

"Um," I started. "I—"

"I go to high school at River Heights High?" she continued. "And I saw your picture in the newspaper, in that article about how you recently helped solve that cyberbullying case at the middle school?"

Ohhh. Finally I realized . . . Lexi wasn't asking me questions. She was just one of those people who made every sentence sound like it ended with a question mark.

"Oh, okay," I said out loud. "Nice to meet you,

Lexi." I smiled, waiting for her to say something else. But she only looked around the coffee shop, as though she was looking for someone else. Okay. Well, maybe she'd simply wanted to tell me that she'd seen the article in the paper. Sweet of her.

"Nancy Drew!" This time it *was* my coffee, and Bess grabbed it and handed it to me over the crowd of people waiting at the counter.

"Thanks, Bess!"

At long last, the sweet, foamy, caffeine-infused drink was all mine. I bent my head to take a tentative sip of the hot beverage when I felt my arm being yanked away from my mouth.

"Omigosh!" Lexi squeaked. "I didn't mean to do that," she said, looking at the tiny puddle of caramel macchiato that had soaked into my white cardigan sleeve.

"That's okay," I said slowly. "Lexi, is there—?"

"Nancy," she whispered, leaning into me. "I need your help."

I glanced at my friends, both of whom were used to this sort of thing randomly happening to me.

"We'll be outside, Nance," George said. "We'll wait for you to finish up and then you can meet us out there?"

I nodded gratefully while Lexi snagged a table that had just opened up by the front door. I sat down and took my first sip of the caramel macchiato ... mmm-mmm. Totally worth the wait.

"What kind of help do you mean?" I asked Lexi, feeling less hostile toward her for spilling my drink now that I'd tasted it.

"Okay." Lexi leaned forward, her necklace—a thin silver chain with a heart locket at the end—dangling over her pale pink cashmere cardigan. "So, two weeks ago I get this e-mail from someone named CandyApple88? At first I thought it was an e-mail from my favorite online makeup store—CandyApple."

I nodded, trying not very gracefully to suck all the rest of the whipped cream from off the top of my drink through Club Coffee's trademark red straw. "But it wasn't?" I asked.

Lexi let out a breath, her eyes darting around the room. "No," she said. "It wasn't."

For a moment I saw her gaze settle on something in the back of the room, and her wide-eyed, sweet, pep-squad look went away for a few seconds. She narrowed her eyes, and her mouth went into a straight line. I turned to see what she was looking at, but just as I did, she began to talk again.

"It was ... this link?"

"To a website," I added.

"Right." Lexi chewed on her bottom lip for a minute, her eyes on my drink.

"Lexi?" I asked.

Her eyes met mine, and her bright blue eyes were now a stunning, practically aquamarine color from the tears she was trying to keep from spilling out.

"What was the website?" I leaned forward, concerned. Suddenly I felt my heart thumping, and that adrenaline feeling that kicks in right when I know I'm about to be on the trail of a huge mystery warmed my arms and legs.

"It was awful," Lexi said softly. "I don't even know why I clicked on it. It was called hatethesegirls.com."

"That's an awful name for a website," I said, taking another sip of my drink. "What was it, some sort of celebrity gossip site?"

"It was a gossip site all right," she said. "All about me and my friends."

That did sound mean . . . but after what I'd learned when I'd helped Bess's younger sister and her friend with her cyberbullying problem, I wasn't surprised. There were all kinds of scary people in the world, and a lot of them seemed to find computers an easy conduit for targeting and hurting people.

I took in Lexi's appearance again. Pretty, blond, I'd imagine popular . . . and wealthy, if her designer handbag and cashmere sweater matched the rest of her wardrobe. It didn't surprise me that she'd be a target of some sort of mean blog.

It was unfortunate, but high school girls could be really vicious. I could only imagine how intimidating an entire group of Lexis would be. Whoever created the blog could have been extremely jealous of all or even just one of those girls, and decided to try to make them feel a little less special by creating something that made them feel bad about themselves.

"What did the blog say?" I asked Lexi.

"Personal things," she said. "Have you ever heard of a burn book?"

I shook my head, curious.

"Well, basically, it's a book where people put pictures of people they know and write horrible things about them. Some are total lies, and some things are . . . well, sometimes there are things that are true. But always mean. Hatethesegirls.com is like an online burn book. It's awful."

"That really is terrible," I admitted. "Have you told anyone? Your parents, or anyone at school?"

"Are you *kidding*?" Lexi asked me. "Why would I draw attention to something like that?"

"Well—," I began.

"It's bad enough that it's out there to begin with? But now the blog posts are getting super personal, and they're really focusing on *me*."

"In what way?" I asked.

"Well, like me being chosen to be the Daughter of River Heights."

"Daughter of River Heights?" I asked, confused.

"Didn't you, like, *go* to River Heights High?" she asked.

Ignore the snark and take a sip of caramel-caffeine deliciousness, I commanded myself. "Lexi," I said after a nice, long drink. "If you want my help—which I haven't agreed to yet—I have to ask as many questions as possible . . . and get as many *answers* as possible."

Lexi sighed. "The Daughter of River Heights is like a mini Daughter of the American Revolution type of thing. Every year, one girl from the senior class is selected by the faculty and her fellow students to be that year's Daughter. It's supposed to be, like, someone with really good grades who exhibits exemplary leadership skills."

"Okay," I said, taking this in. "That sounds competitive. Had you been competing with someone who might have been jealous that you won over her?"

Lexi shook her head, her blond curls bouncing. "There isn't a list of nominees or anything, so no one even knows *who* their competition is . . . or at least, not officially. Everyone just votes, and then the winner is announced."

So that only narrowed it down to most girls in Lexi's class. Suddenly I noticed that Lexi was looking more and more nervous. Bouncing her feet under the table, playing with her necklace—sliding the heart pendant up and down the delicate silver chain so roughly I worried it might break.

"And it's not even that big a deal," she continued. "I mean, my biggest responsibilities are that I ride a parade float on the second day of the River Heights Celebration, and then I present the Mahoney Scholarship Award on the last day of the Celebration. But other than that . . ."

I nodded, though I was sure there were plenty of other girls who would have killed for such a distinction—for their college applications alone. "But what does the Daughter of River Heights have to do with hatethesegirls.com?" I asked.

Lexi stopped moving completely, her already pale skin turning a paler shade of white. "Well, that's the thing," she said. "The author of the blog found out I was the winner even before it was announced."

And that's when I felt the click. Like trying a hundred keys to one lock, and landing on the hundred and first to find that it actually opens the door.

We had a mystery on our hands.

"Lexi," I said, "I'll work with you to find out who is creating this blog on one condition."

"*Anything,*" said Lexi, leaning forward.

"Any question I ask, no matter how weird it may

sound, you have to answer me honestly."

Lexi looked at me, perplexed. And then, perhaps, a little critically. "Okay? But—"

But this time it was my turn to do the interrupting. "It's a deal breaker," I said. "I need you to tell *no one* about coming and speaking to me about this . . . and I need you to make me a promise that you'll tell me the truth about everything that's going on." I'd worked on too many cases where the person I was trying to help had held back information vital to the mystery for so long that it took me twice the amount of time to solve it.

"Okay, then," she said. "I agree."

"For now I have only one more question." I took a huge gulp of my macchiato. "Is there anyone you can think of who would deliberately want to hurt you? Anyone at all?"

Something flashed in Lexi's eyes—nervousness? Regret?

"Well," she said, "I just broke it off with my boyfriend, Scott Sears? He, like, didn't take it too well."

"In what way?" I asked.

"Oh, just—you know . . ."

I could tell there was something off about the way Lexi was talking about Scott. What I couldn't figure out was, what was the source? Lexi or Scott?

"It was a bad breakup?" I prompted.

"Yes," Lexi said definitively—and too quickly, I thought.

"Why did you break things off?" I asked.

Lexi paused. "It was just . . . we'll graduate soon, go off to college. He's going to go to Penn State and I'm going to UCLA. We'll be across the country, and I guess I just wanted to be . . . free?"

I nodded my head, secretly thinking how happy I was that my boyfriend, Ned, and I had both wound up staying in River Heights. But I doubted that if we'd traveled far away from each other to go to different colleges things would have been any different. Sure, we wouldn't see each other as often. But I felt one hundred percent confident in our relationship. There was nothing that could come between us— not even an entire country.

I rustled around in my purse for paper and a pen and handed them to her to write down her contact info, as well as the website address.

She looked at me, pen in hand, hand hovering above the page. And then she started scribbling.

"I'll call you tomorrow," I told her, taking the pen and paper back. At the bottom of the page, I wrote *Scott Sears* and then headed outside to meet my friends . . . and get to work.

BURN BOOK BLOG

"**H**ere it is," George said from behind her brand-new netbook. "Hatethesegirls.com, right?" I nodded, putting my soda down on Bess's bedside table and leaning closer to George. "That's the one."

The background of the website was covered in pinprick-small pink polka dots over a white background. The title of the blog was written in sparkly pink bubble letters—ironic, I thought, considering the content.

Hate these girls? So do we.

Under the headline was a picture of Lexi looking particularly gorgeous in a River Heights cheerleader outfit and her trademark blond waves, surrounded by two other girls in cheerleading outfits whom I didn't recognize. According to the caption at the bottom of the picture, their names were Heather Harris and Aly Stanfield, or "Lexis-in-training," according to the blog's author.

Heather had long, layered strawberry blond hair and the most delicate features I'd ever seen, including a gorgeous spray of freckles dotting her porcelain cheeks. Aly was Asian, with silky black hair to the middle of her back and a killer instinct when it came to makeup and accessories, judging from the picture alone. All three had their arms draped over one another's shoulders. They had huge, sincere-looking smiles spread across their faces.

Unfortunately, the blogger was not only a writer, he or she was apparently an artist, too. All of the girls had drawn-on mustaches and devil horns. I squinted my eyes at the small screen.

"Did you pull it up?" Bess called from inside her never-ending closet, out of sight. "What's it say?"

"It's just how Lexi described—pretty much an online burn book," I said. "Someone is really out to destroy her."

Bess stepped out of her closet. "Um, Lexi? As in Lexi *Claremont*?"

I nodded. "Does that ring a bell with you?"

Bess giggled, going back into her closet. "If you're looking for someone who hates Lexi, you have a long investigation ahead of you," she called out.

"Why?" I asked. "Do a lot of people have a low opinion of her?"

"Try everyone," came Bess's muffled response.

George leaned toward the image on the computer screen. "Lexi Claremont," she said under her breath. "Why does that name sound so familiar?"

"George, how do you zoom on this thing?" I asked, pointing to the picture that had caught my attention.

George pushed a few buttons and touched the keypad lightly, and right away the picture got bigger. It was a little fuzzy—"Low-res," George grumbled.

"Wait a minute," George said, pointing to Lexi. "This is the girl you're talking about?"

I nodded.

"No wonder everyone hates her," she blurted out. "She was Deirdre's Little Sister all throughout high school."

"Lexi is related to Deirdre Shannon?" I asked.

Bess appeared in the doorway. "Nancy, you were just too busy solving mysteries—even when we were freshmen—to remember the Big Sister/Big Brother program at school. As incoming freshmen, we were all assigned a 'Big Sister' in the sophomore class. Mostly it's just a way to have someone introduce you to the school, sort of like a tour guide. Usually people are in touch with their Big Sisters for about a week, and then they go back to their own group of friends."

"But," George interjected, "Lexi and Deirdre became really close. They hung out all through high school. Oh no. Does this mean we have to talk to Deirdre?" she asked, not at all trying to mask the horrified expression on her face.

I laughed. "I don't know yet. But your objection is noted."

George seemed satisfied enough.

I looked closer at the photograph and noticed there was definitely something—or someone—who'd been cropped out. Then I read the caption beneath the photo.

Tired of being taken over by the self-proclaimed hottest clique in school?

Tired of missing out on the chance to date that guy you've had your eye on because you know he only has eyes for blond bombshell (slash airhead) Lexi Claremont?

Thought you had a chance at becoming Daughter of River Heights? Dream on. This girl and her carbon-copy friends rule the school, and we shouldn't have to take it anymore!

The blog went on to suggest that people post their own grievances against Lexi and her entourage—which, indeed, they had done. For eighty-plus pages.

"What do you think about these shoes?" Bess said, flouncing back from her closet in the sundress she'd bought earlier that day and a pair of silver gladiator sandals. She turned to the side and bent one leg at a time at several different angles so that we could get the full effect.

George raised her eyebrows quizzically. "Why are those shoes in style? I don't get it. It's just a bunch of swatches of leather crisscrossing into a huge, tangled mess."

"You haven't been reading the *InStyle*s I've been giving you at all, have you?" Bess frowned.

I cleared my throat. "It's perfect, Bess. But . . ."

"Too much metallic?" she said, touching her silver hoop earrings.

"No," I said, shaking my head. My eyes locked back on that picture of Lexi, Aly, and Heather. "Do you guys notice anything fishy about this picture?"

Bess plopped down on her bed and joined George

and me, looking closely at the webpage. "You mean besides the hideous drawn-on mustaches?" she asked.

"No—there, on the left. It looks like someone was cut out of the picture."

George nodded. "Someone who maybe used to be part of Lexi's clique?"

"And who would do anything to take them down?" Bess finished for her.

"It's a possibility—," I began.

"Wait!" Bess interrupted. "I didn't see it before because I was looking at the picture—but did anyone else check out the time clock on the top right corner of the page?"

"It's a countdown," I murmured. "But to what?"

Bess bit her lip.

"What's up?" I asked her. I'd known Bess long enough to tell when she had a hunch. And her hunches were always something to bet on.

She shook her head. "It could be totally unrelated. But this is the exact countdown to the River Heights Celebration parade."

"That makes sense," I said. "Lexi did mention that it was her biggest role as Daughter of River Heights—to participate in the parade."

"Did you say Daughter of River Heights?" asked Bess, standing up and nonchalantly taking her earrings out of her ears.

I nodded. "You've heard of it?"

"Oh jeez," George moaned, and fell back on Bess's bed, eyes squeezed shut as though preparing for an intense migraine.

Bess sighed. "Stop being so dramatic," she admonished. "I'm completely fine."

"What did I miss?" I asked, looking back and forth from cousin to cousin.

George flopped over on her side. "Don't you remember, Nancy? Senior year, all Bess wanted was to be chosen as our class's DRH. But . . ." She glanced at Bess as if asking permission to finish the sentence.

"But someone beat me," Bess took over.

"Someone beat *you*?" I asked. "But who else . . . ?" I racked my brain for someone who would be a better DRH than Bess. She was smart, sweet, and gracious.

"Deirdre," said Bess, rolling her eyes.

My mouth fell open. Deirdre Shannon had been in our class at River Heights High. I gave most people the benefit of the doubt, even some of the criminals I caught, but Deirdre was one person I knew did not have one redeemable bone in her body. "I don't remember this at all," I told my friends.

"Bess didn't like to talk about it," George said tentatively, rolling over on her side.

Bess dismissed us with a wave of her hand. "It's totally fine."

"But Deirdre doesn't possess *any* of the qualities you'd think they'd want for the class DRH," I argued. "How do you suppose she pulled that one off?"

Bess disappeared back into her closet, and all we heard was a disembodied voice. "Well," she called out, "I hate to break it to you, but Lexi doesn't seem like she's too different from Deirdre, after reading some of the comments on that blog."

I turned my attention back to George's netbook and scanned some of the comments.

"I'm so over this girl. One time she spilled a cherry slushie all over my brand-new white dress just because she was wearing the same one."

"Lexi and her friends are like popularity robots. All they do is wear designer clothes, regloss every fifteen seconds, and glare at other people. Pathetic."

"All I can say is, keep your eye on your boyfriend if Lexi sets her sights on him."

"Lexi Claremont is pure evil."

"Great choice, DRH. The perfect person to represent our student body. HELLO!"

"When is this stupid competition going to nominate someone worthy of the virtues it loves to boast about?? Axe Lexi Claremont from DRH!"

And the comments went on and on from there.

"How could Deirdre and Lexi get chosen for the DRH if any of these comments are true?"

"Easy," said George, fiddling with one of her new gadgets, which looked vaguely like an old model of a Polaroid camera. "It's nothing but a popularity contest. My mother knows the woman who heads the DRH committee—she's a grown-up version of Deirdre. They don't care about leadership, grades, or whatever else they claim to care about. It's all about achieving the perfect curl, or wearing the hottest new designer duds."

I looked at Bess to see if she would chime in with an agreement—after all, she'd once coveted the position. But she only shrugged.

"Well," I said, "I don't know how I'm going to find out who the blogger is with so many people openly hating this girl and her friends. George, can you find out anything online about who the blogger might be, or where they're blogging from?"

George tucked a lock of her short, dark hair behind her ear and grabbed the netbook. "I'm on it," she said.

George was a whiz on the computer. She'd helped me in some way or another with virtually every mystery I'd ever solved, thanks to her tech savvy. But an hour and a half later, Bess and I had resorted to watching reality mystery shows on the television when a frazzled-looking George shut the netbook angrily on the bed.

"Anything good?" I asked.

"Nothing." George scowled.

"Nothing?" asked Bess. "How is that possible? You know more about computers than anyone else I know!"

"Whoever did this is pretty good with computers," George said reluctantly. "He or she blocked the IP—which is not an easy thing to do. I can't even hack through the block. It was tricky—whoever did it definitely knew what they were doing."

I went back to the blog and read a few more entries. After a while, I noticed something. All the comments to the blog posts were just disgruntled people. But the person writing the actual blog seemed to know an awful lot about Lexi and her friends for an outsider.

"Whoever this mystery blogger is," I told my friends, "he or she seems to know Lexi and her friends intimately. And if the things in those blog posts are true"—something I noted to ask Lexi about later—"it has to be coming from someone pretty close to her."

"Like maybe an ex-boyfriend by the name of Scott Sears?" George suggested.

"Maybe," I admitted. I turned to Bess. "Bess, what do you—?"

But when I saw the look on her face, I knew I was in for trouble. She wore an evil grin, one that made her left eyebrow arch and set her dimples deeper than ever.

"What?" I asked, afraid to hear the answer. "Bess, last time you looked at me like that, I wound up being a contestant in a beauty pageant."

George chuckled beside me.

Bess sat on the edge of the bed, looking at me like a concerned mother about to tuck her sick child into bed. "Nancy," she said slowly, "just hear me out. I know that things got a little . . . hairy with you going undercover in that pageant."

I snorted.

"But you solved the mystery!" she reminded me. "And you did it all the way from New York City."

"Cut to the chase, Bess," I urged. "But let me warn you—I am *not* going on a diet this time around."

"You mean *pretending* to go on a diet." Bess giggled.

I shot her a look.

"Okay!" she squeaked. "Just let me explain. . . ."

Back at Boom Babies, I rotated in front of the dressing-room mirror with a frown on my face. I felt ridiculous.

"Come out!" Bess called from outside the stall.

"No," I grumbled. I could hear George's muffled laughter, and I pictured Bess putting her hand over her cousin's mouth.

"C'mon," Bess coaxed. "This is for a good cause—in order to know them, you have to become them. These are the clothes that will get you in with Lexi Claremont and her crew."

I sighed at my reflection in the mirror—short navy blue and hunter green plaid mini. Cream-colored lightweight Italian cashmere sweater. And cute gold strappy kitten heels I doubted I'd last five minutes in without falling down. How could a girl break into an empty house or follow someone soundlessly wearing *kitten heels*? This was definitely not a sleuthing outfit.

I pushed the dressing-room door open and glared at George, whose hand was covering her mouth—but not well enough to conceal the enormous grin that reached all the way up to her eyes.

"Don't. Say. A. Word," I warned.

Bess squealed. "Ooh, Nancy—you look *adorable* in that outfit!"

I turned around and looked at myself in the three-way mirror, surveying Bess's handiwork. "This is all in the name of solving a mystery," I repeated out loud for the billionth time since we'd entered the store.

"Exactly," Bess enthused. "And you couldn't exactly infiltrate Lexi's clique looking like . . ." She glanced at the rumpled jeans and light brown coffee-stained T-shirt that sat on the dressing-room floor. "Well, you."

I frowned. "Are the heels absolutely necessary? You

know I will fall in these. Remember what we learned about my lack of grace from the beauty pageant?"

"The heels stay," Bess said, eyebrows raised in a warning.

"But they make me look so . . ."

"You look like a reject from an hourlong CW drama," George said, finally allowing her laughter to escape.

"It's perfect," Bess agreed.

MEET THE IT-GIRLS

" I 'm sorry, but in order to gain entrance, I'll need your ticket."

I giggled at my boyfriend, Ned, who stood behind the ticket counter in the high school parking lot. "What are you doing here?" I asked.

Ned shrugged. "I was supposed to cover it for the paper, but someone else took the piece. So I thought I'd come by and lend a hand instead."

That was Ned. He was a stand-up guy and the nicest, most honest person I knew. When he wasn't working at his father's newspaper, the *River Heights Bugle*, he was volunteering to help throughout town.

"Well, I'm sorry, sir, I don't have a ticket. You see,

I thought the carnival didn't open until tomorrow," I teased him.

"I guess I'll settle for a peck on the cheek then," he said, smiling.

I leaned over the counter and kissed him, smearing the peach lip gloss I'd borrowed from Bess on his cheek.

"What is this?" he said, wiping the sticky stuff off his face. Then he took in my outfit. "Is this an imposter I'm looking at? What have you done with my girlfriend?"

I explained the latest mystery to him, telling him that I was going undercover as Lexi's friend.

"Lexi Claremont?" Ned asked. "She's already here— over by the frozen yogurt stand."

I rolled my eyes in mock annoyance. "First," I told him, "you're supposed to call it *fro-yo*. Otherwise you're just totally uncool."

"Well, *excuse* me." Ned laughed, running a hand through his close-cropped light brown hair. "And what's second?"

"Second," I said, peering out at the parking lot, which was beginning to look a lot like a real carnival. "I called Lexi last night. She told me exactly where to meet her, and I made her promise not to tell anyone who I was or let anyone know that I'm helping her. If I'm going to get close to her friends, I need them to believe I'm one of them. She agreed—so let's just hope she's a good actress."

"Well, does Lexi Claremont's new friend have time to meet her boyfriend for a hot dog later?" asked Ned.

"She might," I said. "If she can take time off from her fabulous gig helping set up a fro-yo stand."

"Ugh," said a voice behind me. George. "Please stop saying fro-yo. You already look the part, I don't need to hear it too."

"But she looks so adorable!" Bess chimed in beside her, and looked at Ned for confirmation.

Ned held his hands up. "Hey, don't drag me into this," he said. "Nancy looks adorable no matter what."

"Good answer," I said, beaming at him.

"Wow, look at this place," Bess said, letting out a low whistle. "Where did they get the money for all this?"

I looked around. She was right—this was turning out to be a pretty lavish setup compared to past years' events. A bunch of rides had already been put up—a Tilt-A-Whirl, a carousel, a huge Ferris wheel, a crazy-looking roller coaster that seemed designed more for hanging upside down than right side up—and several tents were being set up for games and food. I'd learned from Lexi over the phone last night that all seniors were required to participate in the carnival. Which, I decided, would be a major help to my investigation.

"Mrs. Mahoney," Ned answered. "She donated a ton

of money in her husband's memory. She paid for a lot of the carnival, and she's even presenting one graduating senior with a Mahoney Scholarship Award on Sunday—it's the Celebration's closing event."

"Wow," I breathed. I knew Mrs. Mahoney was wealthy—my dad, Carson Drew, was an attorney, and she was one of his clients. He never said much about any of his clients' personal information, but I knew that her husband, Cornelius, had been sort of a crooked businessman who left her a lot of money when he passed away. Mrs. Mahoney herself was sweet as pie and a major philanthropist in the town of River Heights.

"So." George grabbed my arm. "I have some good news."

"That's what I like to hear," I said, waving good-bye to Ned and walking toward the crowds of people setting up, Bess and George on either side of me.

"I worked all night trying to hack into the IP of hatethesegirls.com," George said in a low voice.

"And?" I asked, getting excited.

"And I was able to find out some information, but not all of it."

"Tell her!" said Bess, her eyes sparkling with excitement.

"The last few blog entries were posted from Club Coffee."

"Are you kidding me?" I asked.

"Nan-ceeee!" I looked toward where the voice was coming from and saw Lexi waving me over from a big white tent.

"Gotta go," I said to my friends. "But Bess—I've got a job for you."

"Anything," Bess said, showing her dimples and smoothing her pretty pink skirt and white V-neck shirt.

I thought for the millionth time how lucky I was to have friends like Bess and George, who offered help anytime I needed it, no questions asked.

"According to Lexi, the entire senior class should be here at some point today. I need you to find a guy by the name of Scott Sears. He's Lexi's ex, and he might have reason to want to sabotage her in some way. I know you can charm him into a conversation—and given this new information about the blog's IP, I'd love to know if he has a penchant for caramel macchiatos."

"Got it," said Bess.

"Nan-*ceeeeeeeeeeee!*" Lexi shouted again.

"I guess I should head over," I said. "But, George— thank you."

"I'm not done yet," she said, holding up her netbook. "I'm going to try to get some more information out of that IP. Whoever set up this blog really knows what he or she is doing. In the meantime, I put up an alert on Lexi's name—so if the blogger posts anything else about her, I'll get a notification on my PDA right away."

"You're the best!" I told her, speed walking over to the fro-yo stand—which, as I suspected, was not the easiest thing to do in kitten heels. I was already regretting not bringing my running shoes with me.

"You guys!" said Lexi, grabbing my arm and pulling me toward her friends. "This is the girl I was telling you about! She's going to help us with the stand. I, um, met her at . . . the nail salon, and you'll totally love her!"

"Oh we will, will we?"

I looked at the source of the sour voice and felt my heart sink. Deirdre Shannon. Of course. Deirdre shook her long, dark waves out behind her and smirked at me. "Nice outfit, Nancy Drew."

I gave a wavery smile and tried to hide my chewed-up fingernails (nail salon!!!). Deirdre and Lexi were with two other girls, both of whom I recognized from hatethesegirls.com. One had strawberry blond hair with expensive-looking platinum highlights—Lexi introduced her as Heather Harris.

The other girl was shorter than the rest. Her name was Aly Stanfield. She was Asian and very athletic-looking. She had the hair I'd always dreamed of having: perfectly straight brown-black hair that was silky smooth and cut in fashionable, razor-sharp layers, the shortest of which was just long enough to pull back into a ponytail.

Once I'd been introduced to all the girls, I

realized that they were wearing the same exact out-fit—a short white tennis skirt and a pink tissue tee—though I did notice that Lexi's shirt was a vibrant hot pink while everyone else wore pastel, even Deirdre. I took a look at their shoes and my spirits sank. They were all wearing silver flip-flops adorned with a tiny rhinestone heart. Ugh. *Waaay* more comfortable than kitten heels! Bess was going to hear about this.

"When Lexi told me she'd made a new friend," Deirdre purred, "I would have never guessed it would be Nancy Drew."

I smiled sweetly, despite the fact that her tone of voice clearly indicated that this was a put-down. "Well, we just . . . hit it off, I guess!" I tried to sound chipper, but it came out more squeaky than perky.

"You two know each other?" Aly asked, applying lip gloss without even using a mirror.

A worry line formed over Lexi's forehead, and she looked at me, expectant. Apparently, she was just as worried about my acting skills as I'd been about hers.

"Oh," I said. "Sometimes you just . . . click with someone, I guess. We didn't even know we'd been classmates until we started talking about RHH."

"Have any of you met Nancy's boyfriend, Ned?" asked Deirdre, looking at me dead-on. "He's quite the charmer. I'll have to introduce you later."

34

I sighed inwardly. Deirdre had been after Ned for as long as I could remember. I knew I had nothing to worry about—Ned had no interest in her whatsoever, and I knew he was devoted to me completely. But I'd be lying if I said that Deirdre's flirtation hadn't gotten to me on more than one occasion. And I couldn't help but remember the line on hatethesegirls.com about Lexi's boyfriend-stealing skills.

"You have a boyfriend?" Heather asked, leaning toward me and running a comb through her golden highlights. "Here?"

"I know, hard to—," Deirdre started.

But at the same time, a petite woman in a pretty gray skirt and matching suit jacket approached the table. "Hello, my favorite girls!" she said in a happy voice.

"Hi, Mara," said Lexi, smiling a very pageant-girl-like smile.

Mara adjusted the cream-colored silk ruffle shirt under her suit jacket and then flipped through some papers she'd attached to a clipboard.

"Aly, honey, your lip gloss," she said, pantomiming wiping off a corner of her lip.

Aly flushed red and wiped away the errant gloss.

"And who do we have here?" Mara asked, looking at me with wide, curious eyes.

"Oh, I—"

"This is my new friend, Nancy Drew," Lexi cut in.

She sure did that a lot. "She's, um, here to help out at the stand? Nancy, this is Mara Stanfield. She's the head of the PTA and the president of the Daughters of River Heights Association. Oh, and Aly's mom, of course."

Mara extended her hand to me and shook it—*ow*—a little too firmly.

"It's nice to meet you, Mrs. Stanfield," I said.

"Please," she said, throwing up her hands, palms out. "Call me Mara. Mrs. Stanfield is my mother-in-law. It makes me feel so old."

"Mo-om," Aly complained.

"Oh, Aly, stop!" Mara shrieked. She was *way* too peppy. I wondered how many macchiatos I'd have to drink to have her kind of energy. Not to mention her heels were much higher than mine, and there wasn't a trace of the pain I was feeling visible on her face.

And then it occurred to me—Mara was Aly's mom? Interesting. If she was the president of the DRH and she'd been involved in the election of one of Aly's best friends as this year's Daughter, did that bother Aly at all? As Mara rattled off a list of fro-yo protocol and detailed the importance of customer service, I studied her daughter.

Aly was gritting her teeth throughout her mother's speech and shifting her weight from side to side. At one point she began to pick at her bright pink nail polish, and then even began to nibble at her nails. Out of all the girls here, I imagined that I would probably get along best with Aly. She seemed a little more down-to-earth than the rest, more reserved. Then I saw Lexi shoot Aly a look. Aly immediately stopped biting her nails and dropped her hands by her sides, and her face flushed again.

I held in my eye roll at Lexi's obvious "It-Girls Don't Bite Their Nails" judgment. Poor Aly. Between Lexi and her mother, I wondered how she ever got a word in. I felt for her, but I also felt something else: a possible motive. Aly didn't seem like the type to write a publicly mean blog about one of her best friends, but being bullied and told what to do all the time could make people do things they wouldn't ordinarily do. I made a mental note to ask Bess and George if either knew anything about Aly Stanfield.

Across the parking lot, I spotted a familiar face. Or thought I did. The man I'd known last as my math teacher had been much heavier, and had more hair. But that pink face and those wire-rimmed glasses were so familiar. Forgetting that I probably shouldn't interrupt Mara's fro-yo server etiquette speech, I blurted out, "Is that Mr. Steele?"

Mara sighed. "Where?"

I pointed to where the man who might be Mr. Steele was heading back into the school building.

"Ah yes," Mara said with a bored expression. "There he is."

"Boy, he sure has changed a lot," I said.

"I'll bet he went on the South Beach Diet," Deirdre remarked, tossing a look at him over her shoulder.

"Well, good for him," said Mara, in a chipper tone that sounded forced. "Hopefully that brings more joy to his life." And then, under her breath, "Although heaven knows why a high school math teacher so clearly disgruntled with his job would choose to head up the carnival committee."

"What?" I asked. That sure came from nowhere!

"You girls are all set," Mara said, ignoring my question. "I'm sure you'll do a great job tomorrow! Right, Alyson?"

"Sure," Aly quipped. "Great."

Once Mara left, the girls and I started wiping down the table and the fro-yo machine parts, counting cups, and assembling the machine. I was reading the instructions for the yogurt machine and had long since taken off my kitten heels when I felt ice-cold fingers grip my wrist.

Startled, I looked up.

It was Lexi Claremont, holding a small square of sky blue paper. And she looked ghost-white with fear.

WALKING ON SUNSHINE

"**A** note?" George asked me.

Ned, George, and I were off the fairgrounds at a picnic table, eating the hot dogs Ned had gotten for us—just far enough away from everyone so that our conversation could be kept private.

I nodded, licking yellow mustard off the corner of my finger. "Apparently, she opened her purse to get her lipstick"—George rolled her eyes—"and she found the note *inside* her purse."

"Creepy," Ned said.

"What's creepy?" asked Bess, plopping down beside George. She helped herself to a hot dog from the center of the table.

"Someone planted a threatening note in Lexi's purse while she was working on setting up the fro-yo booth," George answered for me.

Bess froze with the hot dog halfway up to her mouth. "What did it say?"

I held up the note for her to see.

KEEP SHOWING UP AND YOU'LL BE SORRY.

"Whoa," Bess said, her eyes gleaming with concern. "A gossipy website is one thing. But threatening notes inside her purse? Maybe she should contact the police."

We all traded looks. The River Heights Police Department ran a pretty good operation. But we all knew that Chief McGinnis had bungled more than his fair share of cases. He and I had worked together before—mostly without his knowledge. The way it tended to go was, I found out who committed the crime and where, and Chief McGinnis arrested them once he got my phone call. He was a good guy, but not someone I'd necessarily want solving a crime committed against me.

"I agree—it's übercreepy," I admitted. "And I promise I won't get in over my head."

George snorted, and I shot her a pointed look.

"But," I continued, "there's something about this whole case. It's like every time I'm close to putting my finger on something, that something moves a little to the left."

I examined the sky blue note in my hand. It had been written in black ink, and I could tell the person who wrote it had been writing with his or her nonwriting hand by the way the letters were slanted at odd angles. And there was something I hadn't noticed at first—a black smudge on the very edge of the paper. Not a smudge from the pen, exactly. Something chalkier, almost like charcoal.

I tucked the note in my purse and turned my attention to Bess. "Oh!" I said. "I almost forgot—did you find Scott Sears?"

"Lexi's ex," Bess answered the question written on Ned's face. "And yes, I did." She beamed.

"Uh-oh," said George, folding up her napkin and taking a sip of soda. "He was cute."

"And chatty," Bess chimed in after finally taking a bite of her hot dog. "Fifteen minutes into a casual conversation, he volunteered the fact that his last girlfriend had cheated on him—and that he's glad to be rid of her." She held up a piece of paper with a phone number scrawled on it as further proof of how over his ex-girlfriend Scott really was.

"Lexi cheated?" I asked, a little annoyed. That was sort of a big detail for Lexi to have left out of the story. If that wasn't motivation for taking someone down, I didn't know what was.

Someone's phone started buzzing, and George pulled her PDA out of her pocket. "It's the alert I put out on Lexi's name!" she said. She punched in some keys on her phone, examined it closely, and then looked back at me with a solemn expression on her face. "There's a new blog entry on hatethesegirls.com."

"Can you read it from your phone?" I asked, my pulse quickening.

"I can," George said slowly. "But you're not going to like it." She held her phone out and I took it, Ned reading over my shoulder.

Is Lexi Claremont so pathetic that she had to hire an amateur detective to find out who the author of this blog really is? (A) Yes, or (B) No. If you've guessed the letter A, you win a prize. The Princess of River Heights High has sunk to a new level.

A couple more questions: Who can dish it, but can't take it at all? And who is so vain that one little blog would threaten her place on her throne enough to make her take action? That's right, Lexi Claremont— that would be you. Sad, sad, sad.

"What?" I screeched. "I told her explicitly not to tell anyone about hiring me!"

"Well," said Bess. "Either she's not too good at following instructions, or the author of this blog knows who you are and saw you with Lexi and just put two and two together. Or maybe Deirdre blabbed. She knows you're a detective, and I wouldn't put it past her to mouth off about it."

"Can I just reiterate that I don't like this whole thing?" Ned said. "I don't know, Nance. I know you want to help this girl, but now *you're* showing up on the blog? I'm not sure it's worth pursuing. Remember what happened last time you were online?"

"But don't you see?" I said, the realization hitting me suddenly. "From this blog entry alone, we know more now than we did before."

"What's that?" George asked.

"The blogger has to be someone here. Do you guys think it's just a coincidence that we're all on our lunch break from setting up the carnival, and suddenly a new blog entry goes up?"

"It has to be Scott," said George. "I mean, this *just* went up, and Bess left his side about twenty minutes ago."

Bess shook her head. "I don't think it was him," she insisted. "I talked to him for a while, and he seems really sweet. He seemed more hurt about Lexi cheating on him than anything. I just didn't get that he'd be capable of something like this."

"Of course not," George said, nodding toward the phone number in Bess's hand.

"No," I said, thinking back to the blog entry. "I agree with Bess about Scott. This blog is *serious* into the gossip. It has 'girl' written all over it."

"Guys can be pretty gossipy," said George in a singsong voice.

"Why did you look at me when you said that?" Ned asked, mock-offended.

George laughed.

"Is there anyone in particular you're thinking of, Nancy?" Bess asked.

"Actually, yes," I said. "What if it was someone in Lexi's inner circle?"

"Like Deirdre?" George asked, looking hopeful. Deirdre bugged all of us, but she annoyed George more than anyone else on the planet. She was everything that George hated—entitled, spoiled, rude, and vain.

"Sorry, George," I said. "But I'm thinking more along the lines of someone Lexi's own age. Does anyone know anything about Aly Stanfield?"

I looked around at my friends, all of them slowly shaking their heads.

"The name Aly doesn't sound familiar," Ned said. "But why do I know the name Stanfield?"

"Mara Stanfield," Bess chimed in, as if waking from a dream. When she realized everyone was staring at her, awaiting an explanation, she went on. "She's like River Heights' very own Supermom. President of the PTA, head of the town's Optimist Club, plus she's the head of the DRH. . . ."

"Exactly," I said. "She heads up the DRH."

"And her daughter is a friend of Lexi's?" George asked. "Ouch. That's got to sting a little."

"Seriously," Bess added. She looked at George, then back at me. "Do you know if she's any good with computers?"

"No," I said, holding Ned's wrist out to read his watch. "But I intend to find out. It's time to head back anyway. I'll touch base with everyone later on. And George? Could you—"

"Check on the IP of the latest blog entry?"

I nodded.

"Already on it," she said, pointing toward the high school's computer center.

"Thank you," I said.

"And I'm heading back to the paper," Ned said. "But Nancy, please be careful. Promise me if this looks like it's getting any more serious, you'll leave it to someone else to solve the mystery this time."

"Promise," I said, giving him a peck on the cheek before he headed back toward the parking lot.

Ned was the sweetest boyfriend a girl could ask for, but I knew he got nervous about what I did sometimes. He was only looking out for me, but I had a hunch I was onto something with this Aly Stanfield lead, and I wasn't quite ready to give it up.

Bess and I gathered our napkins and the empty packets of mustard from the center of the table and stuffed them into a plastic bag to take with us and throw out back at the carnival site. As we moved closer, I saw that everything was coming together beautifully.

It looked like a real carnival now—all the rides were completely set up and running (no one was on them yet, so I imagined it was just a few test runs), and the tents were up, each one containing a different game or food vendor that the high school students had arranged. I had to say, it looked really impressive. I was happy for Mrs. Mahoney and the town in general that everyone would have this place to look forward to when it opened tomorrow.

Just then I heard a commotion coming from what looked like a ring-toss booth. Bess and I caught each other's gaze briefly before automatically heading over.

"And I appreciate that," said an upbeat, cheery voice—Mara Stanfield. "But sometimes there is more to participation than just simply *being* somewhere! Right? Right!"

The girl standing next to Mara looked familiar,

though I couldn't quite place her right off. She had hair so black it almost looked blue, and all black clothes from head to toe. Her scowl was dressed up in cherry red lipstick, and she had a bracelet around her wrist that—oh!

"Bess," I whispered. "Do you recognize that girl in the black?"

"I don't know who she is, but I feel like I've seen her before."

"Was it yesterday afternoon, at Club Coffee?" I asked.

"Yes!" Bess said, snapping her fingers. "She was in a booth in the corner and she was—"

"Working on her laptop?" I finished. I didn't know who she was, but if she knew me and had seen Lexi and me together at Club Coffee, it was possible she could have put two and two together.

Bess nodded, and we locked eyes. Without another word, we walked closer to the tent.

"This is a carnival, after all! So let's look like we're having a little bit of fun!" Mara chirped. "Service with a smile!" She knocked on the back of her clipboard with one knuckle, as if for good luck, and then click-clacked away in her heels.

Once Mara's back was turned, the girl in all black rolled her eyes.

Bess and I approached the tent.

"Ring toss?" I asked, indicating the bottles set up in the back of the booth.

The girl in black took in Bess's and my outfits skeptically. I wanted to shout, *I don't normally dress like this! I don't own a stitch of cashmere! And I NEVER wear plaid minis—I'm undercover!* But that would have defeated the purpose. So instead, I extended my hand. "I'm Nancy Drew," I said, "and this is my friend, Bess Marvin."

After a moment's hesitation, the girl took my hand and shook it with a rough squeeze—possibly the only thing she would ever have in common with Mara Stanfield, I thought, stifling a smile.

"I'm Sunshine Lawrence," she said, after shaking Bess's hand.

Bess and I must have raised our eyebrows in tandem—it was impossible not to notice the irony of Sunshine's appearance paired with her name—or else she was used to it, because right away, she sighed and said, "My parents were hippies. Don't even ask."

"She's kind of intense," I said, nodding toward Mara, who had made her way to the cotton candy booth across the way.

"Kind of?" Sunshine scoffed, but I saw a hint of a smile tugging on the corners of her mouth, and I felt her warm up to me immediately.

"So how did you get roped into this?" I asked, playing off the we-hate-this vibe.

"We were required to do something, so I figured

I'd pick something solo that requires little or no attention, so I can read or write during downtime." She nodded to a stack of books and her laptop.

"Smart move," said Bess, playing along.

"What about you guys?" Sunshine asked. "Didn't you already graduate?"

Okay, so she did know us—well enough to know we'd already graduated, anyway.

"Just helping out an old friend," I explained.

As if on cue, Lexi and Heather walked by at that very moment and stopped. They smiled at us and I smiled back, getting ready to ask them if they knew Sunshine. But Lexi's voice interrupted my intentions.

"Well, if it isn't *Emo Girl*," she snarked.

Heather giggled, tossing her long, highlighted locks over one shoulder. "Hi, *Emo Girl*."

My mouth dropped open. Well, this was certainly a side of Lexi I hadn't seen before. I felt Sunshine shifting uncomfortably next to me, and I wanted to do something to help her. Still, I was curious to see where this was all going. I told myself to grit my teeth and let it play out and tried to communicate the same to Bess wordlessly. She looked ready to jump out at Lexi and throw her to the ground. Bess hated bullies more than anything.

"Is it just me," Heather said to Lexi, "or is Emo Girl getting tanner? Are you tanning, Emo Girl?"

Lexi burst out laughing, taking in every visible square inch of Sunshine's pale skin.

"Pale is the new sun-kissed tan," Bess put in, obviously unable to stop herself.

Heather frowned and looked at Bess like she was a harmless new breed of bug she'd never seen before.

"Excuse you?" she said to Bess.

"I'm just saying," said Bess, sizing up Heather and her golden tan, "tanning causes wrinkles." As if to mimic Heather, she scrunched her nose. "And wrinkles aren't super attractive. I'll take my skin porcelain over leather any day."

Lexi shot me a look, as if telling me to control my friend. I elbowed Bess, but only because I wanted to see more of the interaction between Sunshine and the two other girls, not because Lexi wanted Bess to stop talking. If it hadn't been for the case, I would have let Bess continue all day. I loved listening to her put rude people in their places.

"Anyway," Lexi hissed, "your ring-toss stand is *rockin'*." Her beachy waves bounced as she walked toward the stand.

Sunshine took a step back.

"Mind if we test it out?" Heather asked innocently.

"Yeah, I sort of do," Sunshine said in a sarcastic tone that didn't sound nearly as practiced as Lexi or Heather's.

"C'mon, Lex," said Heather, turning and rolling her eyes. "Let's go take a look at that parade route."

Sunshine snorted.

Lexi shot a pointed look at me and then walked away with her friend.

"Friends of yours?" I asked Sunshine once they were out of hearing range.

She slumped back into a chair behind the table. "Hardly," she said.

Bess and I walked behind the table to stand closer to her.

"Are they always that nice?" Bess asked.

"Actually, that wasn't too bad," Sunshine admitted. "It's been like this all four years of high school. I've never done anything to those girls—Aly and I were actually *friends* in middle school. But then when we got to high school she met Lexi and Heather, and suddenly . . ." She trailed off.

I felt awful for her. I had kind of lived in my own world in high school. Ned, Bess, and George had always been my closest friends, and I tried to be nice to everyone else around me. The thought of torturing someone just for fun or to impress other friends—or worse, being the target of ridicule—was almost too much to bear. I started wondering why I'd agreed to help Lexi Claremont in the first place.

But the detective in me wouldn't quiet down.

Something had just been handed to me on a silver platter: motive. What could be a stronger motive for hurting someone than being hurt *by* them for four straight years?

"That must have been very difficult for you," I said carefully. "Have you ever tried to . . . do anything to stop them?"

Bess glanced my way, picking up on my line of questioning.

"Like what?" Sunshine asked, sounding a little defensive. "Girls like that will never change, no matter what anyone does or says."

Bess and I exchanged a look. Validation for writing a spiteful blog? Check. Plus, we'd both seen Sunshine with her laptop at Club Coffee—which, according to the information George was able to hack into, was the same place that the IP address indicated.

I stared at the black laptop behind Sunshine, wondering—and then something else caught my eye. Next to Sunshine's laptop was a larger black box. A cash box, I realized, leaning closer. And on top of it, a little stack of sky blue pieces of paper.

Just like the paper Lexi's note was written on.

SUPAMOM

"Where did you get these?" I asked, holding up a couple of squares of the paper.

Bess's eyes widened.

"The receipts? Everyone has them. Mrs. Stanfield is handing them out with the cash boxes to every vendor. Why? Is something wrong?"

I flipped one of the papers over, and sure enough, there were lines for TOTAL, CASH, and CHANGE printed on the paper.

"No," I mumbled. "Sorry, I was just—that's my favorite color, and I was wondering if you knew where to get them?"

"Sorry," Sunshine shrugged. "I don't know where

they got the paper. But you could always check with Supamom."

"Supamom?" asked Bess.

"Mrs. Stanfield," Sunshine said, laughing. "Or, I'm sorry, 'Mara.' You've really never heard anyone call her that before?"

Bess and I shook our heads.

"It's a joke—president of the PTA, the DRH, skirt-suit wearer, mother of the girl whose aspirations include Harvard, Oxford, and eventually law school? The other mothers in the PTA call her that too, and I guess their kids found out and it just spread. Supamom—like Supermom?"

I laughed, remembering how that very same thought had come to my mind earlier at the fro-yo stand. But something else had caught my attention too. "Wait a minute," I said. "You said Aly Stanfield wants to go to Harvard?"

Sunshine nodded. "And then Oxford. Or Oxford, and then Harvard. Or something. Anyway. It was nice meeting you guys, but I'm going to get packed up and head out. There's only so much work to be done setting up for a ring toss."

Bess and I said good-bye and then wandered away. I pulled out Lexi's note and turned it over. There it was. The printer must have been running out of ink when this one was printed, because you wouldn't even see it if you weren't looking for it—but there, in very faint grayed-out ink, you could see the receipt lines on the back of the paper.

"I don't know how I missed it before," I said, more to myself than to Bess.

"Earth to Nancy Drew!" Bess was waving her hands in front of my face.

"What?" I asked.

"You didn't hear a word I said, did you?"

Oops. "Sorry," I confessed. When I was knee-deep in a mystery, I could sometimes be accused of zoning out and being wrapped up in my own thought process.

"I'm used to it," said Bess, sighing dramatically.

I nudged her shoulder with mine. "Go ahead," I said. "You've got my undivided attention."

"I was *saying*," Bess continued, "that we've got our girl. She has a motive to get back at Lexi and her friends. We even saw her at Club Coffee, and she brings her laptop with her everywhere she goes. Plus, she's got access to the blue paper."

I hesitated.

"What?" Bess asked, surprised. "You don't think it's her?"

"She definitely has the motive and the means to be our mystery blogger. But everyone goes to Club Coffee to get their caffeine fix—and most students bring their laptops with them to do their work. I'd like to get to know Aly Stanfield a little bit better—it seems suspicious to me that she's such a great student and has such high aspirations, yet her own mother didn't endorse her for this year's DRH. Plus, this note," I said, waving it in the air. "It goes way beyond burn book blog gossip. It's a serious threat."

"Maybe it was just meant to scare her," Bess suggested.

"Maybe," I said. "But I don't think we have enough on Sunshine to pin everything on her just yet. And I want to be sure before I go ahead and start pointing fingers at—"

"Nancy!"

I turned to find Lexi standing beside me, all traces of mean girl gone from her face. This girl looked more like a little girl who wanted her mom than a girl capable of terrorizing a classmate for four consecutive years.

"I found another one," Lexi said, handing the sky blue note to me.

I took the note and looked at it. *Call off the detective, or else.* A closer look revealed that this note too had chalky black smudges around the edges—and the reverse side had the same faded receipt lines as the first. I rubbed at one of the black smudges, and it came off on my fingers but stayed on the page as well.

"Lexi, I need to know—did you tell *anyone* about hiring me? Heather, maybe? Or Aly? It's okay if you did, but I need to know."

"Of course not!" Lexi declared. "Like I need anyone thinking I'm a freak show being stalked by some lunatic."

Ohhh-kay.

"Anyway, why were you talking to Emo Girl? Is she a suspect?"

"I was talking to Sunshine," I said, putting emphasis on the fact that I was using her real name, "because I need to look at anyone who might have a grudge against you. I need to rule people out."

"Well, did you talk to Scott?" she huffed. "He's taking this whole breakup thing super harsh."

I could feel Bess holding in a retort beside me, so I responded quickly. "Yes, we're taking a look at everyone who we think might have reason to do this. But my main concern right now are these notes."

Lexi's eyes flitted over to Bess for a minute, and she inched closer to me, speaking into my ear. "Can I talk to you alone for a minute?"

I nodded, holding out a finger to Bess to let her know I'd be right back.

"Look, I'm not trying to be rude or anything . . . ," Lexi started.

In my experience, when people begin sentences

that way, rude is exactly what they're trying to be.

"But," she went on, "my friends have to believe that we're hanging out. And when they see you talking to people like Emo—Sunshine," she corrected, noting my scowl, "it's bad for business. I told them that you were one of us because you said you needed to get close to my friends, but they'll never believe me if you start playing ring-toss with E—with people like Sunshine."

She was right. She was being rude. But back when I was undercover as a pageant girl, I'd met a girl named Portia, who'd taught me that sometimes arguing wasn't worth it. I was just going to have to bite the bullet and play along.

"I'll try to be more covert," I acquiesced.

"Good," Lexi said, satisfied. "I got you an invite to Aly's sleepover tonight? It will be totally fun. A girls' night in to celebrate the Celebration this weekend."

I made my best attempt at a sincere smile at this news. Because like these girls or not, a sleepover at Aly Stanfield's would give me a full-access pass to one of my top suspects.

"I guess I'm . . . sleeping over!"

For whatever reason, when Lexi told me there would be a sleepover at Aly's tonight, I'd mentally blocked the idea of Deirdre being there. But there she was, opening the front door to Aly's house.

"Um," she said by way of greeting, "is that a *pink sleeping bag*?"

"Is this your *house*?" I countered, though my cheeks had warmed at her comment. It had been a long, long time since I'd had a sleepover with anyone other than Bess and George. We were so close that we felt comfortable wearing anything we wanted to bed—even our old cartoony flannel PJs. And we'd either share a bed or sleep on the couches downstairs. Were sleeping bags passé?

I knew I should have asked Bess more questions! She'd loaned me a cute pink rhinestoned velour tracksuit—supposedly the "hottest new trend in loungewear"—that she'd gotten for a song at an outlet mall just outside River Heights.

"Are you going to invite me to come in?" I asked Deirdre's scowl.

She rolled her eyes, opened the door wider, and made an impatient "hurry up" gesture with her manicured hand.

When I walked in, I suddenly realized why my sleeping bag was probably unnecessary. As large as the Tudor-style home looked from the outside, it looked infinitely larger inside. Like, mansion-size. There was a long, winding staircase done up in marble. Oriental rugs ran down long hallways. Even the foyer chandelier was impressive—what looked like real crystals hung teardroplike from the gleaming gold embellishment on the ceiling fixture.

I took my shoes off right away and placed them on a shelf with several other pairs. I hadn't realized how dirty my tennis shoes looked until I saw how perfect and clean the others were.

Deirdre had already deserted me while I was gaping at the palace laid out before me, so I followed the giggles and squeals coming from upstairs, and when I entered what I was now sure was Aly's bedroom, I was struck once again by the size and elegance of it all. The bed was a maplewood, intricately carved four-poster with a deep maroon-and-gold-colored comforter dotted with several golden throw pillows. The walls were painted the same deep maroon as the comforter—and several felt Harvard pennants were framed and hung throughout the room, along with artful black-and-white posters of the campus. The floor was gorgeous dark hardwood accented with cream-colored rugs here and there, which gave the otherwise very adult-feeling bedroom a cozy feel.

There was a walk-in closet to the left of the door, where Lexi, Heather, and Deirdre were flipping through Aly's designer-label-laden wardrobe and trying on various selections from the rows upon rows of shoes in every shape, heel, and color imaginable.

In the center of the closet was a makeup station the size of a kitchen island that contained all my favorite makeup brands—plus, I noted, a large selection of CandyApple glosses and sparkly shadows.

I wondered what Mr. and Mrs. Stanfield did for a living, other than Mara being "Supamom."

"Welcome!" Aly said from a corner of the room I hadn't even seen yet—on the opposite wall from the closet. She was sitting at her enormous flat-screen computer, checking her FacePage, and she swiveled her chair to smile and wave at me. We noticed at the same time that we were wearing the same exact outfits in different colors—mine was pink and Aly's was charcoal gray.

"Glam Couture?" Aly guessed.

"What else?" I giggled, once again glad to have someone like Bess in my life.

"I'm glad you could make it," Aly said. And once again, I got the feeling that if we'd met at a different time in our lives, we could have really been friends. I wondered how she fit in with the other girls, how she'd found them or how they'd found her.

"Yeah," said Deirdre, emerging from Aly's closet with a fistful of nail polish. "We're overjoyed."

Heather and Lexi came out with nail polish remover and what looked like various creams and sharp-looking manicure tools.

"Oh," Aly said. "Are we doing manis now?"

Lexi stared at her for a moment, and a look passed between them.

"I just thought," Aly said, "maybe we'd wait to do them before the movie so that our nails can dry while we're watching."

"Al," Lexi purred. "You know I put together sleepovers better than anyone. Why don't you let me handle the planning?"

Aly shrugged. But suddenly, unexpectedly, Heather spoke up. "I agree with Aly. Face masks and makeovers now, then we go downstairs for pizza, then nails and the movie in the screening room."

Screening room? I thought. As in, home movie theater. Seriously, what did Aly's parents *do?*

There was an uncomfortable moment when we— except for Deirdre, who was lounging on Aly's bed, texting away on her phone—just looked between Lexi and Heather. Apparently, Lexi wasn't used to anyone opposing her suggestions.

"I agree," I said to break the silence, but I also thought this plan would give me a chance to get a feel for a dynamic among the girls—and maybe even pull Aly aside to get her candid thoughts on her friends. Then, when everyone was downstairs doing their nails and about to watch a movie, I would run upstairs to look through more nail polish selections and take a peek at what was on Aly's computer.

"Cool!" Heather chimed in. And, with a sideways glance at Lexi, "It's settled then."

After having my face smeared with green goo and wearing it around for twenty minutes, only to wash it off and then have layer upon layer of makeup caked on my face by Heather, I had begun to realize something: Sleepovers with these girls were always group-centric. I doubted I'd be able to get Aly alone for enough time to dig up any real dirt about her friend-ship with Lexi.

I also realized that being around these girls was like a real-life burn blog. All they did was gossip, talk about their classmates' hideous sense of fashion, and discuss who was dating whom behind whose back.

"Did you hear that Mr. Steele had, like, a mental breakdown over the summer?" Lexi asked. "I heard he was in the loony bin for months. My mom said he had to beg the school board to let him back."

Aly wasn't so much into the gossiping, I noticed, but occasionally she'd come out with something that surprised me.

Such as, "Did you hear that Tara Rockefort left school for a month to get a nose job?"

Lexi, Heather, and Deirdre giggled, tilting their heads back like it was the funniest piece of gossip they'd ever heard. "And guess what she told people she was out for?" Aly went on. "I'll give you three choices: A, she went to visit her sick grandmother in Chicago. B, she had a bike accident and was in the hospital recovering. Or C, mono. Who wants to guess first?"

While the girls answered her question, I felt my blood go ice-cold in my veins. A, B, C . . . it was almost exactly what had been written on hatethesegirls.com earlier today! I thought back to what George's PDA had displayed on-screen, back to those first couple of sentences: *Is Lexi Claremont so pathetic that she had to hire an amateur detective to find out who the author of this blog really is? (A) Yes, or (B) No. If you've guessed the letter A, you win a prize.*

Could it just be a coincidence? And if not, why would Aly use the exact wording, almost as if she knew Lexi was trying to find out who the blogger was?

Lexi shot a look at me, eyes worried. Looked like we'd had the same thought.

"What's your guess, Nancy?" Aly asked.

I looked up, startled. "My guess?"

"It's been narrowed down to sick grandmother and mono. You're the tiebreaker!"

Oh! Phew. "Um, grandmother?"

"Ding ding ding!" Aly called out. "We have a winner. She totally lied about having a sick grandmother and got a nose job instead. How gross is that?"

"I'm hungry," Lexi announced. "Can we *please* go downstairs and ask your mom to order us pizza?"

"Mara's not home, and neither is Dad," said Aly. "They're at some fancy fund-raising event. But we can go down and order it ourselves."

Ummm, okay. So Aly called her mother "Mara" and her father "Dad." That was certainly interesting enough to follow up on. Could Aly be so angry with her mother for endorsing Lexi for this year's Daughter that she refused to call her "Mom?"

"I'm hungry too," I chimed in, eager for a chance to have a peek at Aly's computer alone (and take off the pounds of makeup that had recently been added to my skin).

Once the pizza was devoured in the "great room"— a room I could only describe as palatial—the girls sifted through the pile of nail polishes to pick their colors. Deirdre chose blood red, then went back to texting (according to Lexi's taunts, they were going to a new boyfriend, whom Deirdre was being uncharacteristically quiet about). Lexi chose a pretty raspberry pink, Heather chose hunter green—"this season's hottest color"—and Aly chose a soft baby pink.

This was my opportunity.

"Aly, do you mind if I go upstairs and check out some of your other colors? It's hard to match a color to my skin tone."

"True," Deirdre said derisively.

"Of course!" said Aly. "Do you want me to come with you and show you where they are?"

No!!! "No—I mean, thank you. But I remember where they are. And I don't want to hold you up—you guys get started on your manis and I'll be back down in a few."

When I got to Aly's bedroom, I turned on the light in the walk-in closet where the nail polish was, but decided to keep the lights to the rest of the room off, just in case anyone happened to walk by. I sat down at Aly's computer. Her desktop wallpaper was, surprise, the Harvard crest, and everything was saved neatly into several folders.

I looked behind me, making sure no one had suddenly decided to join me, then pulled the flash drive George had given me out of my pocket. I plugged it into the computer's USB port and followed the instructions George had given me earlier in order to copy everything on the hard drive into the flash.

I watched the "copying" progress bar as it crawled across the screen. "Come on," I whispered, wondering how long it would be before someone noticed that I'd been missing for a while.

I jumped when I heard a creak in the floorboards and froze, ready to make a dash for the closet at the next sign of noise—but no other noise followed the first. *Guess it was just house noises*, I thought.

While I was waiting, I figured I'd do some poking around. Doing something always made me less anxious than sitting still and waiting.

I went through various folders and saw nothing helpful. Papers dating back to the beginning of high school. A flow chart of her GPA in each class and what GPA she needed overall to become valedictorian. Plus, downloaded applications to nearly every school in the Ivy League.

The girl was driven.

I clicked on the web browser and searched through her history, but it had recently been cleared. *I wish George was here!* I thought, closing the browser.

Then I came across an Internet icon labeled "Alymail."

With one more glance behind me, I opened it, ignoring the thumping sound in my chest.

I could feel it . . . I was going to find something in that file that didn't look good for Aly. But when the folder finally opened, a little box popped up, asking for a password. Unlike any other file on her computer, this one was password-protected.

Suddenly the room was flooded with light.

BRICK BY BRICK

My heart nearly leaping from my body, I whipped around in my seat ... to find Mara Stanfield standing in the doorway of her daughter's bedroom.

"You girls, always on the computer!" She shook her head. "I thought you could use a little light."

As soon as I caught my breath and talked my body out of the heart attack it had begun to have, I sputtered out a thank-you and explained that I'd just been checking my e-mail.

I glanced at the flash-drive status on the screen: COPY COMPLETE. *Phew.*

"Where are the other girls?" Mara asked.

"Um . . ." I ejected the flash drive on the screen, and then pulled my borrowed shirt sleeve over the flash drive sticking out of the USB, careful not to allow Mara to see what I was doing, and pulled it out of the computer. "I think they're painting their nails downstairs—I just came up to find a different color and—"

"Oh!" Mara exclaimed. "Let me help you pick. I love fashion and all things related!"

I followed behind her to the closet, tucking the flash drive neatly into the deep velour pocket of my track pants. I noticed for the first time how dressed up Mara was. She wore a long black cocktail dress with a glamorous deep V neckline and a slit up the side to her knee. Silver strappy heels poked out from underneath, and her neck was adorned with a huge diamond pendant necklace that shone in the track lighting of Aly's closet. Her hair was pulled back into a perfect chignon, with a few well-placed wisps hanging delicately down.

"So," I said, as Mara sifted through the polish bottles, "your home is really lovely."

"That's so sweet!" she said, making brief eye contact. "What a polite young lady you are. Carson Drew's daughter, correct?"

"Yes," I said. "Nancy." A lot of people in River Heights knew my father from his work as an attorney in our sleepy little town. "You know," I continued, "before I saw Aly's room, I hadn't realized that she was so interested in going to Harvard."

Mara picked up a bottle of nail polish, a deep, smoky purple. "Here it is. This is the one! It will look absolutely *perfect* with your—"

But she was interrupted by the sound of a huge crash downstairs—glass, from the sound of it, and then nothing but the sound of a group of girls screaming their heads off.

We dropped everything and ran downstairs to the great room, where Aly was standing, pink-faced, in front of a huge broken window, tears in her eyes.

"What happened?!" Mara nearly screamed as she took in the sight of broken glass sprinkled over the carpet, coffee table, and part of the couch.

"I don't know—," Aly sputtered. "There was a crash and then—glass spraying everywhere—and—"

"It was a brick," said Lexi, as if in shock. Her eyes were wide, her face ashen.

"Omigosh!" Heather exclaimed from her hiding place behind the couch. "I can't believe anyone would do something like that! What is *wrong* with people?"

"Okay," Mara said. "Everyone stay calm and go upstairs. I'm calling the—"

"Wait a minute," I said, surveying the room. "Where's Deirdre?"

"She went outside to call her boyfriend!" said Heather. "Do you think she's okay?"

"I'll go check on her," Mara said. "Go upstairs."

Lexi and I lingered while everyone else filed upstairs. Lexi pointed to an object below the window, in the middle of a pile of shattered glass. I carefully tiptoed over, shook the glass off the brick, and examined it. Around it was a rubber band, and beneath the rubber band, a message. Written on a sky blue piece of paper.

"What did it say?" Bess said, a slight waver to her voice.

The next morning Bess, George, and I had gathered at George's house so I could fill them in on all the details before the Celebration officially began.

Once we were all sitting at the breakfast table, George invited us to help ourselves to a basket of fresh-baked muffins, scones, and bagels her mother had left out for us. Everything smelled delicious.

I pulled the note out of my purse, as well as the flash drive. I handed the flash drive to George and the note to Bess.

"'Next time, there will be no warning,'" Bess read aloud. "What's *that* supposed to mean?"

"Nothing good," I admitted. "But things have definitely escalated. Whoever is doing this could have seriously hurt someone last night. We've got to figure out who's behind all this before . . . I don't even want to think about what else could happen."

"We can do this," said Bess. "How many mysteries have you solved, Nancy? And you're not in this alone. You've got us."

I nodded, then looked at George. "I looked through a bunch of files on Aly's computer—and they should all be there. I didn't find anything but progress charts, goals, and applications to Ivy League schools. But there was one file that was password-protected."

"I'm on it," George said.

"Isn't that pretty incriminating by itself?" Bess asked, taking a bite of a blueberry muffin. "I mean, this girl wants Harvard bad, right?"

"True," I said.

"And her mother has the ability to put something impressive on her college applications."

"This year's Daughter of River Heights," George confirmed.

"Right," Bess agreed. "But she passes over her own daughter and helps her daughter's supposed best friend, who, let's face it, doesn't exactly exemplify the qualities I would think they're looking for."

"My thoughts exactly," I said, breaking off a piece of a cinnamon-raisin scone and stuffing it in my mouth. "But we were at Aly's house, and she was in the room when the brick was thrown through the window."

"She could have an accomplice," suggested George.

"But would she have had someone throw a brick into her own window?" I asked.

"If she was working with someone else," Bess put in, "maybe she did it to throw you off her track. Or at least Lexi."

"Possibly. Someone like Deirdre," I said, thinking it over.

"Deirdre?" Bess asked. "But do we really think she's capable of throwing a brick through a glass window?"

"Not really," I agreed. "No matter how nasty she may seem, I don't think she'd actually want to physically hurt anyone. But the weird thing is . . . she was the only one of us outside the house when it happened."

George perked up. If the situation hadn't been more serious, I would have laughed. Not so secretly, I think she's been waiting for Deirdre to be the culprit for a long time.

"Where was she?" George asked. "I thought you were all at the sleepover together?"

"We were," I said. "But apparently, she went outside to call her boyfriend right before the brick got thrown through the window."

George nearly choked on the lemon poppy-seed muffin she'd been munching on. "Are you kidding me? First of all, *what* boyfriend? Second, how can that be a coincidence? She totally has something to do with this!"

"George," I started.

But Bess interjected. "Actually, Nancy, I think this time my cousin might be right."

George looked at Bess in obvious surprise. "You do?"

"Well," said Bess, standing and brushing crumbs off her lap. "Deirdre was last year's Daughter of River Heights, right?"

"Right," I said. "That's what you said earlier."

"So maybe she doesn't like the fact that her 'Little Sister' is catching up to her. Look at it this way—how do you think Miss America feels when she relinquishes her crown to the new Miss America? It's got to be hard being the *former* best at something, even if you're not competing against anyone directly."

"Probably like a has-been," George joked. We all knew George's opinion about beauty pageants.

"But that's true," Bess countered. "What is next after you win a big distinction like that? I'm not saying that the DRH is comparable to Miss America. But think about it—Deirdre loves competition like nothing else. What does she have now?"

I considered that for a moment. But it was still

difficult imagining Deirdre doing anything violent, like throwing a brick through a window. One thing was for sure: If our blogger did have an accomplice, I was going to find out about it, and fast. Before anyone really did get hurt.

I looked at the time on my PDA: 7:52 a.m. The carnival opened at nine, and we were supposed to be there prepping for the big opening by eight.

"Yikes, you guys—we're going to be late."

"I'm ready," Bess said, with a flourish. She wore her opening-day outfit, the one we'd spent forever trying to find at Boom Babies a couple of days before—and it looked gorgeous on her.

Watch out, Scott Sears, I thought.

"Let's get out of here," George declared, grabbing Bess's keys.

Bess grabbed them back. "Not a chance," she admonished.

"Whatever," said George. "But Nancy?"

"Yes?"

"Make my day, and prove that Deirdre had something to do with this."

I laughed. "I'll see what I can do."

"A *brick* through a *window*?" Ned asked from behind the ticket counter. "Nancy, I really don't like this. You could have been hurt."

He stretched his hand out over the counter to grasp mine and squeezed it, concern filling his warm brown eyes.

"I know," I said. "But if I don't help Lexi find out who is behind any of this, someone definitely *will* get hurt."

"And there's no one else who can solve mysteries in this town?"

Behind us, some of the River Heights High faculty were setting up a red ribbon for Mrs. Mahoney to cut before they opened up the carnival to the public. Mr. Steele was in the background, barking orders at everyone and making sure that everything was running smoothly.

He did not look happy. I remembered those looks from when he'd passed back an exam I'd flunked because I'd been out late the night before, trying to solve a mystery.

"You put up with it because you love me," I said to Ned, smiling.

"You make me nervous because I love you," he said. "But if I know anything about you, I know that when you set your mind to something, you will not be stopped."

"You won't get an argument from me on that one," I agreed.

"All I can continue to say, then, is be careful. And watch out for Mr. Steele. He's on the warpath today."

"I noticed," I said, looking at the chaos taking place on the fairgrounds. "What's going on here, anyway?"

"Mrs. Mahoney had very specific instructions about the way she'd like everything to go." Ned shrugged. "I guess they're trying to do everything they can to accommodate the person who made all of this possible."

It really was amazing. Everyone was bustling around, and the smell of hot dogs, funnel cake, cotton candy, and sausage and peppers made my mouth water. There were rides going, the carnival music was flowing, and game booths were set up everywhere you looked. You'd never have believed that just days ago, this was an ordinary high school parking lot.

"It's time!" Mr. Steele barked through a megaphone.

"See you soon," said Ned.

We'd agreed to meet up at the end of the day for the big fireworks display that would be happening as soon as the sun went down. It was going to be the only thing that would get me through my day at the fro-yo stand with Lexi and the other girls.

I leaned over the counter and gave him a peck on the cheek, then joined the others in front of the giant red sash that had been set up before the carnival entrance. Mrs. Mahoney, a slight, kindly-looking elderly woman with silver hair and wisps of bangs, stood with Mara Stanfield, who was holding a pair of scissors.

George and Bess joined me in the crowd.

"This is some turnout," George said.

"Much bigger than any year before," said Bess. "Which is great for the scholarship fund."

"What scholarship fund?" I asked.

"Remember?" Bess said. "The Mahoney Scholarship Award—you're the one who told me about it. Isn't that one of Lexi's duties as this year's Daughter? To present the award?"

"Oh, right!" I said, remembering. "It's the last duty that she'll have to carry out for the Celebration. Tomorrow is the parade, and Sunday is the scholarship presentation. But what does that have to do with this year's turnout?"

"Mrs. Mahoney is putting up enough money for one full college scholarship to the winner. But the other three candidates get to split the ticket sales money from the carnival."

"Wow, that's actually pretty cool," George chimed in.

"*Very* cool," I said. "I can't believe I forgot about that scholarship. I'd love to get my hands on a list of the candidates. Bess, today I want you to shadow Scott, see if you find him scribbling notes on any sky blue papers. My instinct tells me he's not our guy—but I'd still like to know more about him."

Bess grinned sheepishly. "Well, I *guess* I could do that."

George rolled her eyes. "I want a job!" she said.

"I'm going to be working at the fro-yo booth with Lexi and the rest—I'll try to get more information out of Aly, see if there's any strain on her relationships with any of the other girls. But George, if you could get into that password-protected file and hang around Sunshine Lawrence whenever you're done, that would be a huge help."

"Done," said George.

"Ladies and gentlemen!" Mara's voice boomed out over the crowd. That woman definitely did not need a microphone to be heard. "Welcome to the 80th annual River Heights Mahoney Celebration. This year we honor Mrs. Mahoney and her late husband, Cornelius."

I heard someone snort behind me, but when I turned around, there was only a row of people looking attentive and interested in what Mara was saying.

"The Mahoneys have been a huge part of the history of this town, and we owe Mrs. Mahoney a great deal for her philanthropy and the goodwill that she has made sure to spread throughout our beloved town."

Mrs. Mahoney turned a bit pink and swatted

Mara's doting words away like a fly buzzing near her ear. But her mouth was turned up in a smile. I grinned just looking at her.

"In fact, we owe all of this"—Mara gestured toward the carnival—"to the Mahoneys and their generous donations to our schools. Before Mrs. Mahoney cuts the ribbon, I want to remind you all that there will be a fireworks display this evening starting at approximately nine o'clock. Tomorrow there will be a River Heights town parade, featuring this year's Daughter of River Heights, Miss Lexi Claremont."

She paused while people in the audience clapped. During the applause, I looked around at the sea of faces around me, searching for any sign that someone was unhappy at the mention of Lexi's name. But only Sunshine, who I already knew disliked Lexi—and with good reason—was scowling.

"Finally, to close out this year's Celebration, we will be handing out the Mahoney Scholarship Award, which will offer one of four candidates the opportunity to get a full four-year college scholarship. The money made from your ticket sales here will be split among the runners-up."

More cheers.

"And without further ado, I would like to hand the ceremonial scissors over to Mrs. Mahoney, so that she may cut the ribbon and the carnival will be open for business!"

At this, the younger kids in the audience cheered loudly. I anticipated seeing many children in near sugar comas sleeping through the fireworks display by the end of the evening, judging by all the candy-selling food stands I saw being set up yesterday.

"I just want to thank the citizens of this town," Mrs. Mahoney said into the microphone in a shaky voice.

I felt the kids go still. I could read their minds: *Not another speech. Give us candy!*

"It's an honor," Mrs. Mahoney continued, "to be here to witness all the people I saw first as children grow up to be fine, upstanding young citizens. It is my honor to do my part in bettering this community in any way possible. I look forward to this weekend as much as any of you."

Mara handed Mrs. Mahoney the scissors and held the red ribbon taut for her to cut the fabric.

Mrs. Mahoney made the cut, and the ribbon fluttered delicately to the ground in two pieces.

The Celebration had begun.

FUEL TO THE FIRE

"This. Is so. Boring," Deirdre said, leaning over the counter, playing with select strands of her raven hair.

"I'll bet it would be less boring if you actually lent a hand," I chimed in, trying to tame my stream of fro-yo into an elegant spiral. It was my seventh one of the day, and it had turned out just like the others— in strange, awkward squiggles that were barely contained by the cups we'd been given to pour into.

"I want sprinkles!" said the kid in front of me, whose head barely cleared the counter.

"Me too!" said his brother.

"I'm sorry," I said, wiping my brow with the back

of my hand. "We don't have sprinkles, but we do have fresh-cut fruit and granola."

Kid Number One stuck his tongue out in obvious disgust. Kid Number Two shook his head in disdain. *I'd rather have sprinkles too,* I wanted to tell them. Their mother paid, gave me a fleeting smile, and then struggled down the fairway juggling her children's hands, two oversize stuffed giraffes, and a shiny green balloon in the shape of a bullfrog.

"I don't know," Deirdre drawled. "Looks like you've got it covered." She smirked at me.

I only sighed. So far, all I'd managed to do was follow or give instructions at the fro-yo stand. I thought we'd have a slow morning, considering that it was, well, morning, but I'd underestimated the heat, and we'd been swamped the whole time.

"Hey babe," a deep male voice said behind me.

I turned around, a look of barely contained surprise on my face as a guy with dark, brooding eyes and an outfit to match wrapped his arms around Deirdre. Hello, Deirdre's new boyfriend. Where were you at, say, 9:52 yesterday evening?

"This is Josh," Deirdre said, introducing him to Lexi first, then Heather, then Aly, and finally, with a flip wave of her hand, to me.

Josh nodded at each of us. I noticed that this guy was not the type that Deirdre normally went for—

if her never-ending, not-even-close-to-contained crush on Ned said anything about her type. Whereas Ned was All-American, clean-cut, warm, and charming, Josh fit more into the "bad boy" category.

He was tall, with shaggy dark hair and a lanky body, and scruffy stubble covered his chin and jawline. He wore loose, vintage-looking jeans with a studded belt and a tight-fitting white T-shirt. And by the way he looked at all of us, I doubted he cared to be anywhere near the fro-yo stand with his new girlfriend.

"When're you gonna get outta here?" I heard him whisper to Deirdre.

Deirdre pouted at us. "You guys, this is, like, so unfair. I'm the only one here with a boyfriend, and I could totally be doing better things than hanging out here."

And that was when I noticed something odd pass between Aly and Heather. Right after Deirdre said she was the only one with a boyfriend, Aly got a weird, uneasy look on her face and glanced at Heather. Heather looked . . . the only way to describe it was furious.

And Lexi, who'd just broken up with Scott—a bad breakup, as I recalled—looked oblivious to the tension around the rest of the group. She simply poured the world's most perfect cup of fro-yo, handed it to the teenage girl waiting in line, smiled, and said, "Have a great day!"

What was all *that* about?

But before I could even begin to think about it, the screaming started. At first it was only a few people. And then the screams got louder, and more people were joining in. It was maybe thirty seconds before I could make out what they were saying, but it felt like an eternity.

Finally I heard it. One word, over and over: *Fire! Fire! Fire!*

And then I saw it, licks of flame rising up above the crowd. I traded looks with the other girls before whipping off my apron and sprinting toward the center of the screaming mob.

Bess appeared at my side, fire extinguisher in hand and Scott beside her, also with a fire extinguisher. It wasn't as bad a fire as I'd thought—though big enough to cause alarm in such a large crowd with so many fire hazards. But with the help of Bess, Scott, and their two fire extinguishers, the fire was out in a matter of seconds.

"What happened?" I asked Bess breathlessly, once the crowds had dispersed.

Bess shook her head. "I was talking to Scott here at his corn-dog stand." She pointed to the booth right next to where the fire had broken out. "And all of a sudden, the whole sausage-and-peppers cart went up in flames!"

"Is everyone okay? Was anyone hurt?" I asked.

"No one was hurt," Scott cut in. "Everyone got away in time—but what we can't figure out is how the fire even happened in the first place."

Two high school guys—I assumed the ones manning the sausage-and-peppers grill—were wiping down the fine white dust that the fire extinguishers had left on everything in their path, and Mara and Mr. Steele were bickering behind them, discussing whether or not they should call the fire department.

I walked toward the charred, blackened soot, looking to see if there was anything out of place, anything that could have caused the fire.

Scott held up an arm, blocking my way. "Be careful," he said, lowering his arm slightly.

I nodded and inched a bit closer. Something smelled . . . off. I could smell the burning and the smoke, but there was something else I detected too. Something that didn't belong anywhere near the gas stove that had been cooking the sausage and peppers.

"Does anyone else smell that?" I asked.

"Yes," Bess said, looking down at her new dress with a frown. "I'm going to smell like charred onion for weeks."

"No, I'm serious," I said, waving both Scott and Bess over toward the black mess.

"I was being serious too," Bess complained. "And my hair—is that . . . gasoline?"

"Lighter fluid," Scott said with certainty. "It's the same stuff my dad uses to pour over the coals when we barbecue at home. But there's no reason to use it on a gas stove."

"Someone had to have thrown the fuel on this fire to ignite it," I said. "I'm sure of it. This was no accident."

"Who would have done something like that?" Scott asked.

Bess and I traded looks. Good question.

"So no one knows who did it?" Lexi asked.

"Nope," I answered. "We questioned the two guys who were manning the stand, and they had no clue. One of them had just left to get a soda from a nearby stand, and the other was so busy he lit up a third burner that they hadn't turned on until right then."

"So the lighter fluid could have been on there from the very beginning, and it was just luck that they hadn't used that burner yet," Aly said.

"Exactly."

Lexi shuddered. I could tell that she was thinking what I'd been trying not to think this whole time:

What if the fire was related to the threats toward Lexi? It seemed unlikely, just coincidence, but something told me not to rule it out just yet.

I walked toward Lexi, about to try to soothe her nerves, but something attached to the corner of our tent caught my eye. Something flapping in the breeze.

I stopped midstep and squeezed my eyes shut, hoping that I was just imagining things. That I was overtired and I hadn't just seen what I thought I'd seen. But when I opened my eyes, it was still there. A small, sky blue note taped to the tent pole of our fro-yo stand.

I snatched it off the pole right away and immediately identified the telltale smudged black ink and the too-faint receipt lines printed on the other side. I braced myself, then looked at the slanted writing.

You're not listening to me, Lexi. Show up at that parade, and you'll regret it. You thought the brick flying through your friend's window was scary? That's nothing compared to what I've got planned for you tomorrow.

I tried to control the look on my face, because I knew Lexi was watching me. But the truth was, these notes were getting more and more serious, and I really was starting to get scared. Maybe Ned was right. Maybe it was time to involve the police.

"What does it say?" said a fragile voice behind me.

"It's just more of the same," I said, forcing a strong voice. "I don't think you should even read it, really. It's just more like the others, and I—"

Lexi pulled the note out of my hands. Not roughly, like she was grabbing it away. She just took it gently. Like we were passing a note in class.

When she looked back up at me, there were tears in her eyes. Despite everything I'd seen about Lexi— her vanity, the way she'd treated Sunshine, her impatience toward me earlier— all I wanted to do was wrap my arms around the girl and tell her that everything was going to be okay. Trouble was, I wasn't sure that was true.

"Why would someone do this to me?" Lexi whispered.

"I have no idea," I admitted. "Lexi, I'm not going to stop trying to find out who this person is, or why they're doing what they're doing. But I think it's time to involve the police. This has escalated to a level that—"

"No!" Lexi shouted, anger adding strength to her voice. "If we do that, they won't let me do any of the things I'm supposed to do this weekend. The parade, the scholarship presentation, all of it will be ruined!" Her voice was gaining power with every word. "And

I am *not* going to let some jealous *loser* scare me out of taking what I deserve!"

I tried to reason with her. "Lexi, we're not just talking about some gossip website anymore. These notes, and that brick—that was real life, all of it. This is getting a little beyond my reach."

"Then quit," Lexi said simply.

"What?"

"I said, quit." Lexi folded her arms over her chest.

I bit my lip, weighing my options. It was clear that Lexi didn't want to involve the police. And to be honest, I didn't blame her. Even though the sabotage was clearly escalating, I'd solved enough mysteries in this town to know that involving our local police department on a hunch wouldn't necessarily ensure Lexi's safety more than my own investigation. Still, I wasn't thrilled about the idea that I was the only person who could help in such an extreme situation.

I blew out a breath and placed my hand on my hip, hoping to look more authoritative than I felt. "Okay, Lexi," I said. "Let's make a deal."

She eyed me warily.

"Give me until the end of today," I continued. "If I can't at least find a strong lead suspect by then, you agree to alert the police as to what's been going on."

She opened her mouth to protest, but I cut back

in. "Give me today," I said again. "And then we'll talk about it."

Lexi looked doubtful, but I could tell that she was happy that I'd given her a deadline to look forward to.

"How many suspects do you have now?" she challenged.

I counted in my head. There was Scott Sears—the guy with whom Lexi claimed to have had a bad breakup. But was a bad breakup enough motive to write threatening notes and throw a brick through a window? Besides, Bess claimed he seemed happy as could be. But something about the way Lexi talked about the breakup unnerved me, and I wasn't willing to let him go as a suspect yet.

There was also Aly Stanfield. She was an insider in Lexi's group and would have plenty to spill on the blog. Plus, she had a motive—being passed over for this year's DRH by her own mother. Suspect number two. But I was stuck on the brick going through her own window. Would she really have asked her accomplice to do that, even if it would divert attention from her? Possibly.

Much to George's amusement, I wasn't counting Deirdre out as a suspect either. She'd been the only one outside when the brick had been thrown into Aly's living room the night before. She claimed to have been speaking with Josh. But could I get him to confirm that?

And then there was Sunshine Lawrence. More motive than anyone else we'd spoken with, plus she'd been on her laptop at Club Coffee when we'd first seen her. She had more than enough reason to want to destroy Lexi and her clique of friends.

"So far, we have four," I told Lexi. "But we need to find out more to be sure."

"Four?" asked Lexi, incredulous. "There are four people you've spoken with who would want to hurt me this way?"

I shrugged. "Like I said, we need to find out more, but—"

"Names," said Lexi bluntly.

"What?"

"Names," she repeated. "Of the suspects. I want to know who they are."

"I can't do that," I said firmly. "There's no reason for me to incriminate anyone without being sure that they've done something wrong. And besides, if you go after any of the people I tell you about, you'll scare them off and blow the whole investigation."

"Fine," Lexi groaned. "But Nancy? End of the day today."

CURSED CARNIVAL

Bess and I met up at the picnic tables on the outskirts of the carnival, where we'd all had our hot dog lunch yesterday.

"Scott has been a perfect angel the whole time," she said, a starry look in her eyes.

"I suspect your personal feelings are beginning to cloud this investigation," I said, laughing.

She played with a lock of her golden hair, twisting it around her index finger. To most people, this would be a sign that she was acknowledging how right I was. But I'd known her since we were kids, and I knew better.

"Bess?"

"Mmmm?"

"Spill it," I said.

She sighed and dropped her wound-up lock of hair. "Sometimes I hate how well you know me."

"Spill," I repeated, with more urgency this time.

She examined her manicure. "Well," she began. "There is this *one* weird thing that's been happening."

I stared at her, urging her on, but she only continued to stare at her nails.

"Bess!" I shouted.

She jumped. "Jeez, *okay*," she said. "It's just that . . . some people who have been buying the corn dogs at Scott's food stand have been complaining of feeling a little . . . well . . . queasy afterward."

My jaw dropped. "Like food poisoning?" I asked.

"Like queasy," said Bess. "I mean, who knows if it's the corn dogs? Although it might seem a little suspicious, I guess. If he were, you know, a suspect."

"Which he is," I reminded her.

"Okay, fine." She looked up and then looked directly at me. "It's possible that it's food poisoning. And if we're leaping to conclusions, I suppose it's possible—logistically—that if Scott is running the food stand, he might be sabotaging the food. But Nancy, I'm serious. I honestly don't think he's our guy. The look on his face when people started complaining about the food—he looked absolutely heartbroken. He takes great pride in those corn dogs."

I nodded, taking this all in. Something just didn't feel right about this whole thing. Writing a burn book blog about a group of popular girls was one thing—and the notes definitely took the danger quotient up a couple of notches. But a fire at the sausage-and-peppers stand, and possibly now a food poisoning case at the corn-dog stand? How were those incidents related to the sabotage of Lexi Claremont? If anything, it felt like someone was trying to sabotage the carnival itself. But who would want to do that—and why?

My phone buzzed in my pocket—it was a text message from Ned.

COASTER. NOW!!!

I had no idea what the text meant, but I knew my boyfriend, and he wouldn't have written something so cryptic had there been time to explain.

I shot up and grabbed Bess, not even stopping to explain as I pulled her back toward the carnival.

The closer we got, the louder the crowd became. Soon we could hear screaming. Terrified screaming.

I looked up at the roller coaster as we approached and realized it wasn't moving. The people at the top were screaming the loudest—they were also hanging upside down.

I spotted Ned and ran over to him. "What's going on?" I asked.

Ned shook his head. "It's stuck—and the machine operator has no idea how to fix it."

Bess marched over to the man who was trying to keep the customers in line calm. "Who is in charge of fixing this ride?" she demanded.

"Look, miss, we're doing everything we can. We'll have it fixed in no time."

"Let me rephrase that," said Bess. "Tell me who is in charge of fixing this ride, or I'll spread a panic throughout this carnival that will have you fired before you can even change your mind."

The big, burly guy she was talking to held up his thick hands in submission, then gestured to a wiry man past the gates of the roller coaster, who was frantically running his hands across a large, gray box at the base of the ride.

Bess moved past the burly man quickly, ignoring his plea of, "Miss, you can't go back there!" and waving me away as I called out to be careful.

I moved closer to see what she was doing and, against the burly man's orders, followed her to the machine operator.

"What's going on?" Bess demanded, digging around in her purse.

"Who are you?" the man replied, staring at Bess in all her breathtaking beauty.

"Is the ride broken?" I asked, distracting him.

"We're working on it," he tried to assure us. But the screams were sounding more panicked, and I could tell from the look on his face that this guy was out of his comfort zone.

"Look, maybe we can help," I said. "What went wrong, and how long have those people been stuck up there?"

The man sighed, scratching at the stubble on his face. "Too long," he admitted. "Fifteen, twenty minutes." He ran his hands over the large gray box again, seeming to search for something only he knew existed.

"Where is it?" Bess asked.

He looked at her, stunned.

"Where is what?" I asked my friend.

"The lever," Bess responded. "It's what keeps the ride going *and* what stops it. And it should be right"—she placed a finger on a narrow slit on the box—"here."

"Who are you again?" asked the man, dumbfounded.

At that moment, Bess pulled a travel tool kit out of her purse. "Someone," she said, holding up the kit, "who might be able to save your job."

More screams erupted from the top of the coaster as the cars lurched forward a fraction of an inch and then stopped. I couldn't imagine how those poor people felt!

"I—I have no idea how this could have happened!" the man said, frantic. "Whoever did this must have done it on purpose. Without the lever, there's no control—and there's no damage to the box. Whoever did this had to have taken the box apart quickly, and they knew exactly how to extract the lever."

"Let me try it," Bess said, pushing him aside with her shoulder.

"Miss, I appreciate your help, but this could be dangerous."

"Trust me," I intervened. "You want her help."

I knew more than anyone how good Bess was with machines. She might look like a sorority girl who knew nothing more than the new "it" color this fall and what shoes to wear with which length pants, but she was the savviest person I knew when it came to fixing any type of machinery. She was a whiz when it came to cars, in particular, but she knew her way around a toolbox when it came to almost any other type of machine.

Bess opened the travel toolbox and shifted around some tools I'd never even seen before. Before we knew it, she'd taken the entire box apart and had wedged a screwdriver into a small place between two round, jagged gears. Then she pried the screwdriver back and forth and finally seemed to hit something. Soon the screaming rose and then fell silent as the roller coaster slowly began to move again.

Bess shimmied the screwdriver every couple of minutes, allowing for the ride to stop and for each carful of terrified-looking people to get out. Half an hour later, the ride was completely empty, and she'd shut it off for good.

Bess wiped machine grease onto a towel that the wiry, wide-eyed ride operator handed her, and I was just about to tell her how amazing she was when something out of the corner of my eye caught my attention.

I squinted toward where the movement had come from and saw that it was a figure in a black hoodie moving among the shadows between the rides. I couldn't tell who it was—he or she (the hood was covering the figure's head, making it impossible to tell if it was a man or a woman) was too far away and moving far too quickly, but one thing was for sure: Whoever this person was, they'd been watching us.

Without a word, I headed off after the figure.

I ducked into the dangerous areas behind the rides, earning plenty of glares from other ride operators as I went. It seemed the figure was always ten steps ahead of me—rounding a corner just as I'd cleared the last.

Whoever this person was, they were taking me for my very own ride.

It was growing darker outside, as clouds threatened to open up and release a torrent of rain, and every sound and every shadow became more and more ominous.

For a moment I thought I'd lost the person in the black hooded sweatshirt. But then I saw a flash of black at the front entrance of the school. I thought I heard my name being called behind me, but there was no time to turn around. I sprinted to the front doors of the school and yanked them open, the suddenly menacing sounds of the carnival rides fading as the doors closed behind me.

Silence.

I looked around. The hallways were dark, and there were so many corners of the building, the hooded figure could have been anywhere. My heart slammed against my chest as I took in the deafening noiselessness with the realization that I was utterly alone.

I looked outside, where people were oblivious to the danger that might be lurking around, oblivious to people who might be starting fires and rigging rides. And then I looked forward. I had no choice. Whether or not the hooded figure had anything to do with Lexi's case, they were obviously trying to hide.

As I walked through the linoleum hallways, the kitten heels that Bess had insisted I wear again today echoed loudly around the building. I cringed, my heart skipping a beat, and slid them off. I laid them on the floor and crept along in my bare feet.

When I passed the first classroom, I paused at the door. I could feel my pulse beating erratically in my throat and tried to swallow it into submission. The deeper into the school I walked, the darker it became, and now I could barely see my hand in front of my face.

I reached out toward the door and grasped the brass knob. I felt a chill run up my spine that I was sure had nothing to do with the frigidity of the doorknob. Slowly I twisted the classroom door open. When it was fully open, I let out a breath I hadn't known I'd been holding, and my hand groped desperately along the walls for a light switch.

I felt a wave of warm relief wash over me as my fingers grasped the switch and light flooded the room. I scanned the room frantically, looking for the lurker with the black hoodie, and found—to my relief or horror, I couldn't decide which—that no one else was there.

Just in time for the lights to cut back out.

I gasped inadvertently and edged my way back out of the classroom. At this rate, I'd have a heart attack going through each and every classroom this way . . . especially without any lights.

Just a couple more rooms, I told myself. I stood as still

as possible in the middle of the hall, willing my eyes to adjust to the darkness surrounding me. I listened to every creak and moan of the old school building, my ears searching out any noise that resembled a footstep, or even a breath.

When I was certain there was no one around me, I walked forward, keeping my left hand on the wall of lockers to help guide my way. I walked along on my toes, still in bare feet, trying to make as little noise as possible so I could better search out any sounds in the building that could be human.

The moaning creak of an opening door caught my attention, and I hustled toward the sound. *And what exactly will you do when you find this mysterious black-hooded person?* I asked myself. But I'd come too far to chicken out, and it was too late to think about the consequences now. I pushed the thought to the back of my mind.

Suddenly lights flooded the building. Every classroom and every hallway was lit up so brightly that I had to squint my eyes to readjust my vision.

A cold hand clapped down on my shoulder.

I gasped, whirling around.

"Nancy!" George said. "It's just me!"

I put my hand over my heart and gulped in some breath.

"George," I croaked. "You scared me half to death!"

"Sorry," she said. "But I've been looking for you everywhere, and when I finally ran into Bess, she told me that you ran off toward the school. Listen, we need to talk. I was able to get into Aly Stanfield's password-protected file and—hey. Why are you barefoot?"

I looked at my feet, having completely forgotten that I'd taken off my shoes. And there it was, lying right next to my left foot. At first I thought my eyes were playing tricks on me. An aftereffect of standing in the dark for too long. But the longer I stared, the clearer it became.

A crumpled-up piece of sky blue paper.

I bent to pick it up and carefully unfolded it—but before I even opened it, I knew what I would find. Black smudges, all over the paper.

"Another note?" George asked.

"This one's blank," I said. "But look." I held it up to her.

"Same black smudges," she said.

"Same black smudges," I echoed. "George, I don't know why, but I think that the person writing the blogs and the notes is the same person who started the fire and removed the lever on the roller coaster. We need to solve this mystery, and fast."

"Well," said George tentatively, "that's what I was trying to tell you."

"What's that?"

"I've been working on Aly's password-protected file all afternoon—and I was finally able to get in."

"How?" I asked, excited.

"Easy." George smirked. "I guessed her password."

"You *guessed* her password?" I said incredulously. George knew even less than I did about Aly Stanfield. And the only thing *I* knew, even after the sleepover, was that Aly was a hard worker who wanted nothing more than to get into . . .

"Harvard," I said out loud, smacking my forehead with the palm of my hand.

George only smiled. "Bingo," she said. "Boy, I sure could have used you about two hundred passwords ago."

"George, I'm such an idiot—I should have known!" But she only shook her head.

"Doesn't matter now," she said, eyes gleaming. "I think we may have found our girl."

SECRETS, SECRETS EVERYWHERE

Bess, George, and I huddled around the computer screen in the computer lab.

"It's a series of saved IM conversations between Aly and some guy named Brad," George explained. "They were careful not to get into any specifics, but they're definitely hiding something, you can tell."

I scanned the saved conversations.

> ALYCAT: I DON'T LIKE THIS. U KNOW I HAVE 2 TELL HER.
>
> BRAD33: PLZ! ALY, YOU MADE A PROMISE.
>
> ALYCAT: SHE'S GOING 2 FIND OUT. I'M NOT KIDDING, U HAVE 2 DO SMTHNG. IF U DON'T . . .

BRAD33: WE'LL TELL HER. PROMISE.
ALYCAT: WHEN?
BRAD33: SOON. 1 WK, TOPS.
ALYCAT: 4 THE RECORD, H8 THIS.

"Okay, so Aly is definitely hiding something," said Bess.

"She sure is," I said. "The question is, what? And from whom?"

George leaned back in her computer chair and crossed her arms. "Aly has the DRH motive, and now it looks like she's got something to hide—and an accomplice. Combine that with her drive to get into Harvard. Nance, she must be at the top of your list."

I tilted my head, as though seeing the IM chat from another angle would help me to somehow find the hidden meaning. "It's suspicious for sure . . . but there's nothing in here that says she's talking about keeping something from Lexi. And we don't even know who Brad33 is—or if Brad is even his real name."

"That one was dated a month ago," George interjected, closing the chat and opening a new one. "But this is the most recent one."

Bess and I leaned forward, peering at the screen.

BRAD33: Y R U IGNORING MY TXTS?
BRAD33: ALY?

ALYCAT: U TOLD ME THIS WOULD B OVER BY NOW.

BRAD33: AFTER ALL THAT'S HAPPENED, WE HAVE 2 KEEP THIS BTWN US

BRAD33: U CAN'T TELL ANYONE

BRAD33: U PROMISED.

ALYCAT: HOW CAN I TRUST ANYTHING U SAY NOW? I CAN'T EVEN BELIEVE U!

ALYCAT: I'M DONE LISTENING.

BRAD33: U'LL REGRET IT, ALY. DON'T DO THIS.

ALYCAT: I'M GOING TO TELL HER.

[ALYCAT HAS SIGNED OFF]

"Whoa," Bess breathed. "If that one was a week ago, even if Aly didn't make good on her promise to spill this secret . . ."

"Which is possible," I reminded her.

"Which is possible," Bess repeated. "But what if Aly was working with someone to get back at Lexi for the DRH nomination, but then things got too serious and she changed her mind? If her accomplice wasn't ready to stop, it would cause a rift between them and this whole conversation would make perfect sense."

I tapped my nails on the table, thinking.

At the sound of George's phone buzzing in her pocket, she reached in and pulled it out. "Another alert on Lexi's name," she read, then looked up at Bess and me. "It's from hatethesegirls.com."

I looked at my friends, my mouth forming a grim line.

"Go ahead," I told George. "Bring it up on the computer."

In seconds the website came up, and the familiar pink bubble letters sparkled on the screen. I couldn't help but notice that the banner on top of the page no longer boasted a picture of the three girls—both Heather and Aly had been cropped out. Whoever the author was, he or she had begun to set his or her sights on Lexi Claremont and Lexi Claremont alone. This year's Daughter of River Heights smiled out from the screen, oblivious to what the words below her read.

I read the most recent post once, twice, three times in a row, my eyes sweeping the page for any possible clues as to the blogger's identity.

Poor little Lexi Claremont. Thinks she has it all, and doesn't know it's all about to come crashing down on her Gucci shoes. Because, you see, being a member of the Daughters of River Heights is all about prestige and honor. And girls who lie and steal to get what they want have nothing to say about either of those virtues.

You think you have it all, Lexi? Think again. Even the people who are close to you know your dirty little secrets. And pretty soon, all of River Heights will know who their "daughter" really is. Good luck at tomorrow's parade, Lexi Claremont. You'll need it.

Just as I was about to point out the myriad of clues buried within the blog post, I had a thought.

"George, can you check the IP time stamp?" I asked, looking at the time on my PDA: 4:52 p.m.

"No problem," said George, tapping her fingers along the keyboard. After a few moments, she looked up at me. "Four forty-eight p.m.," she said. "And the IP says it's coming from the high school's wireless network."

I smiled.

"I've seen that look before, Nancy Drew," Bess said, raising an eyebrow at me. "What do you know that we don't?"

I had a theory, but I didn't want to make an accusation without confirming the facts first. But that required the help of my friends.

"George," I said, "can you go back to the blog post that appeared the day we saw it for the first time, right after Club Coffee and shopping for Bess's dress? Can you get a time stamp on that one too?"

George began searching, the *tick-tick-tick* of the mouse scroll moving faster and faster.

"And Bess," I said, locking eyes with her, "do you

by any chance still have your receipt for that dress you're wearing?"

Bess looked confused for a moment, then dug through her purse, pulling out a pretty silver wallet. "Of course I have my receipt," she said. "I *always* keep receipts."

That's what I was counting on, I thought as she pulled out a neat stack of tissue-thin papers and began flipping through until she found the one she was looking for.

"Got it," George said, tracing a fingertip along the words on the computer screen.

"Here you go," said Bess, handing me the receipt from Boom Babies.

I compared the time on the blog post to the time on the receipt—same day, twenty minutes apart. Which, if George's research about the IP was correct, meant that we were in the same place as the blogger—Club Coffee—when one of the entries was posted.

I hurriedly explained my theory to my friends.

"Do we remember who else was in there with us?" Bess asked, tucking the receipts neatly back into her wallet.

"Well, it was pretty crowded," I said, closing my eyes to try to conjure a mental image of the shop. "There were a bunch of kids from the high school who had just gotten out of school. In fact, it was so crowded we couldn't find a seat."

"Sunshine was there," said George, scooting forward in her chair excitedly. "Remember, Nancy? You thought you'd found a seat, but it turned out that Sunshine was just ducking under her table so that she could—"

"Plug in her laptop," I finished for her.

We looked around at one another.

"So Sunshine is a strong suspect," I said. "She was in the right place at the right time—with her laptop—*and* she has the motive to want to take Lexi down, but what do you think she'd have on Lexi to threaten her with before the parade?"

"Unless that was an empty threat, just a fake-out," George suggested. "To scare her."

"True—but the blogger already knows that Lexi hired me. Wouldn't that indicate that she's already pretty scared?"

Bess bit her lip. "Okay, so who else?" she asked.

"Lexi was also there when we were," I said, "because that's where she first approached me. But do you guys remember if anyone was with her?"

"Like Aly?" Bess asked.

I nodded my head, hopeful.

"Sorry," said Bess. "I don't remember. I was on a bargain-shopping high."

"And I was rifling through my gadgets," George admitted.

"And I was suffering from major caffeine with-drawal." I sighed, sitting in one of the twirly com-puter lab seats and allowing the full weight of my body to sink down into it.

I was suddenly aware of how exhausted I was. I'd barely gotten any sleep the night before at Aly's sleepover, and today had felt like a marathon relay race. Every time I finished putting out one meta-phorical (or even literal) fire, my friends and I had another one to deal with.

It was as if someone was toying with us the same way they were toying with Lexi. I thought about Ned's caution—that this one might be over our heads. And my muscles *did* ache from the tension of walking through the school in such a panic. My fingers were permanently numb from pouring (and missing) too many cups of fro-yo. My feet were kill-ing me from those stupid kitten heels I had to wear in order to fit into this ridiculous popular girl's little club. I was tired, and just about ready to give up.

And then it hit me.

I sat up straight, suddenly feeling wide awake. If I felt this way after only one day of trying to fit in with these girls, and run at their pace, imagine how some-one doing it for several years would feel. Imagine what someone would be willing to do to get back at Lexi Claremont, just for being her.

"We really need to solve this mystery," I told my friends. "I refuse to be outwitted by some bitter blogger who wants to destroy this town's carnival just because they have it out for one overprivileged girl."

George looked at me as though I'd lost my mind.

Bess gave me a timid smile. "Nancy?" she asked. "Are you okay?"

"I'm better than okay," I said, standing and wincing as I put my blistered feet back into my kitten heel shoes. *Oh, well,* I thought, *that's what calluses are for.* "So we've got to talk to Sunshine and Aly—and anyone who could have been there with Lexi the day she hired me."

"What about Scott Sears?" Bess asked.

I laughed. "I think your boy is in the clear," I said. "You were right before. This has *girl* written all over it."

INTERROGATION TIME

First we decided to take inventory of the fro-yo stand. Deirdre Shannon, her new leather-clad boyfriend Josh, and Heather were all missing—and Aly Stanfield was typing away on her PDA.

"Where did Heather and Deirdre go?" I asked Aly.

"To—quote—take a break—unquote," Aly replied.

"Did they leave together?" I asked, feeling guilty for having left Aly to take care of the fro-yo customers all by herself.

"Nope," said Aly, shooting me a quizzical look. "Deirdre left about half an hour ago with Josh—and Heather left about five minutes later. Why?"

"No reason," I said. Except that everyone had left

the booth just in time for another blog post to go up. Not to mention the fact that Aly herself was typing on a PDA that looked more than equipped to post an entry from.

"Checking your e-mail?" George asked, clearly reading my mind.

Aly put a hand on her hip and sighed. She addressed me. "Look. I knew I'd get stuck doing all the work—no big deal and nothing new. But I'd really appreciate it if you and your friends could find someone else to chat with. I'm taking a practice SAT test online, and I don't need the interruption, okay?"

"You can do that?" I asked, rushing to Aly's side. I peered over her shoulder at the phone clasped in her hands. "What question are you on?"

"Excuse you," Aly said, moving the phone away. "But this is my personal, private property. You really do seem to have a thing about invading other people's stuff, don't you?"

I wrung my fingers together, my heartbeat quickening. "What do you mean?" I asked.

"Please," Aly said in a way that practically screamed *You're irritating me!* "My mother totally saw you on my computer last night."

"Oh," I said, glancing at my friends. I was surprised that Mara had ratted me out—after all, she'd offered to pick out a nail polish color for me and everything!

"Is that all? I was just checking my e-mail."

"Find anything good?" she asked, raising an eyebrow.

"Not really," I said. "Just spam."

"Interesting," said Aly. "Because our Internet service has been down for days. A guy from the cable company is coming next week to fix it."

"Oh?" I said worriedly. I'd just blown my cover! "That's so strange. . . . I could have sworn that—"

"Actually," George interrupted, "it's not all that strange. Internet is going in and out at our place too. Probably the strong winds that have been blowing through town off the water. Must've been a fluke."

I tossed George a grateful smile.

"Whatever," Aly said, sounding bored. "Just go ahead and leave so I can finish my test?"

She didn't have to ask me twice.

On our way to visit Sunshine at the ring-toss booth, I voiced my opinion about Aly's Internet problems. "If her Internet hasn't been working for a few days, that would explain the IP coming from Club Coffee."

"And from the school," said Bess.

"But," I said, playing devil's advocate, "I saw her phone, and she really was doing an SAT practice exam online—plus, she was on question thirty-seven. No way she'd have gotten that far *and* posted to the blog too."

"Maybe she minimized it and switched between them?" Bess ventured, sidestepping a pigtailed little girl with glittery stars and rainbows painted on her cheek.

"But isn't the SAT a timed test?" I asked. "Would the practice test let you pause it, even if just for a minute, without making you start the whole thing over again?"

"Good question," said George. "I'll look that up once we're done interrogating Sunshine."

I raised my eyebrows in surprise. "Interrogating?"

"Nancy, I know you think that Aly is the most likely culprit here," George replied. "But we have more evidence to back up the accusation that Sunshine is behind this. Remember, we never even saw Aly at Club Coffee that day."

I glanced at Bess, only to find that she seemed to be in agreement with George. I knew that they both had a point, but something about this still didn't feel settled. I couldn't help but feel that Sunshine was merely the most convenient answer, and that we must have been overlooking something.

As we walked through the center lane of the carnival, all the scents mingled in the air, making my mouth water. I realized I hadn't eaten since breakfast, and it was already nearing six o'clock! I looked at the crisp, warm funnel cakes dusted with fine white confectioner's sugar. The sausage-and-peppers cart had been reassembled with a new burner and smelled yummier than ever. Even the hot dogs . . .

I turned toward Scott Sears's booth, but it was vacant, and the food had been half put away. There was a young-looking high school boy packing what was left of the condiments into a big brown box.

"What happened?" I asked him. "Decide to call it quits for the day?"

He screwed up his face and looked around. "Don't tell anyone—I'm supposed to keep it secret. But it was food poisoning," he said. "Please don't spread it around, though. Mr. Steele doesn't want word getting out that the carnival is cursed or anything—especially after the roller coaster and—Hey!" he said, looking at Bess. "You're that girl who fixed the ride!"

Bess blushed.

Even though she should have been used to it by now, she didn't like too much attention being directed toward her for things like this. It was simply something she enjoyed doing, and she happened to be very good at it. Besides, she obviously had something else on her mind—something far more important than saving the coaster. Well, according to her.

"What about Scott Sears?" she asked the boy.

He scrunched up his nose as though he'd just smelled something gross. "He was, uh, sampling the merchandise, apparently. He got sicker than anyone else. He's going to be okay, but he was taken to the hospital for dehydration."

"Oh, that's awful!" I said. "I hope he feels better."

"*See,*" Bess hissed in my ear as we continued walking. "I *told* you he wasn't a suspect."

"You were right," I conceded as we walked away.

The moment we approached the ring-toss booth, Sunshine quickly glanced at us, turned around, and slammed something shut behind her.

"Hey, Sunshine," I asked. "Slow day?"

"Why do you think I chose the ring toss?" she joked. "No one lines up for that when they could ride the roller coaster of death, or sample some delicious poison corn dogs."

My blood ran cold. If she were the culprit, would she have brazenly admitted to knowing about two things that she was responsible for—especially since the corn-dog stand scandal seemed to be under wraps?

"How did you know about the corn-dog stand?" Bess asked menacingly.

Sunshine rubbed her stomach. "Made the mistake of having a few bites," she said with a queasy look on her face.

"But you didn't finish it?" I asked. "Why not?"

Sunshine rolled her eyes. "I'd never had one before,

so I tried one. Those things are disgusting!"

I leaned against the counter of the booth—as much to take the pressure off my feet as to get closer to the object of my intrigue. "So what have you been working on?" I asked, nodding toward her laptop.

"Oh," Sunshine said lightly, color creeping into her pallid cheeks. "Not anything, really. Just messing around."

"Really?" I asked. "On what?"

"Just this thing," she said. She'd regained her composure and crossed her arms over her chest now, challenging me.

"Online?" I asked.

Sunshine laughed. "What's with the sudden inquisition?" she asked. "If you need to borrow a computer, there's a labful inside the school."

I looked toward my friends, nodding them away. If I was going to get anything out of Sunshine, it would have to be a one-on-one conversation. Considering her experiences with Lexi and her friends, I imagined she wasn't too into spilling secrets to groups of girls—particularly because, at the moment, I resembled a Lexi look-alike.

"Sunshine, have you ever heard of a blog called hatethesegirls.com?"

She looked to the side dubiously, then back at me. "Nooooo," she said slowly. "Should I have?"

I shrugged. "I just thought you might have."

"Why?" she asked. Her brows knitted together, and she bit her lip in an uncharacteristically vulnerable way. "Does it say anything about me?"

She turned to her laptop, pulling up the Internet browser and immediately typing in the address I'd just given her. There was a tense moment when her entire body went rigid . . . and then she burst into tears.

Or at least, I assumed they were tears. Her shoulders shook and her hands flew to her eyes, wiping tears away. It wasn't until she turned around and I saw the gleeful look on her face that I realized she wasn't crying. She was laughing.

"Oh, Nancy . . . you didn't think . . ." She burst into a hearty laugh.

"Okay," I said, growing impatient. "I don't get it. Fill me in on the joke."

Sunshine's jubilant tears had smeared the thick black eyeliner around her pretty eyes, and she carefully traced a finger underneath to tidy the smudge.

"It's just . . . you think I did this, don't you?"

I shrugged, feeling not a little bit foolish. Sunshine clearly hadn't known about the blog. I knew how to tell when people were lying, and this had been an honest reaction to that blog.

Sunshine tilted her head and looked at me. The

hysterical laughter had died down, but there was still a trace of a smile on her face. "Why would you think I'd do something like this? Just because some bratty girls called me names in between classes?"

"Well," I said, "actually, yes. You're telling me you've never wanted to make their lives difficult? Never wanted to out them to the world as the artificial, mean girls they are?"

"Sure I have," she admitted. "They made my life really difficult at River Heights High. But look at this thing." She gestured to the blog that was up on her computer screen. "Does this look like my style?"

I took in her black dress, the black intentionally ripped tights, the red Mary Jane platforms. Her pale skin, red lipstick, and ever-present black-string bracelet with the red charm. No, this website definitely was not her style. I doubted the word "pink" was even in this girl's vocabulary.

"You're right," I admitted. "I'm sorry for accusing you. It was just—had I been in your shoes, I might have wanted a little revenge myself."

She shrugged. "I get it," she said. "But would you have acted on it? I mean, trust me. There are plenty of times I'd like to see the prom queen fall from grace. I mean, send a mass e-mail telling everyone that her Chanel handbag is a knockoff? Sure. Tell the world about her new guy? That would be sweet. But unlike Lexi Claremont and the sheep who follow her, I know that life goes beyond high school. She might rule the school now, but wait until I get out there and become a famous research scientist and rid the world of infectious diseases. I'll be accepting the Nobel, and she'll be reliving her high school glory days in her head. A blog is too easy. Still, thanks for telling me about it. I'll be sure to keep an eye out to see what happens."

Great, I thought. Here I was, trying to solve the mystery for Lexi, and I was only fueling the popularity of the blog by running my mouth about it to people who already hated her.

"Well, thanks for talking to me, Sunshine. It's cool that you have such a mature perspective. I wish the author of this blog and all those notes shared your opinion."

"Notes?" she asked.

Oops! "Oh, just . . . nothing to worry about. Thanks again."

I had to contact Bess and George. Next and final stop: Aly Stanfield. I was sure of it now. All we had to do was prove she'd been in Club Coffee the day I'd met Lexi Claremont, and we would be in business.

FIREWORKS

"**N**ancy! We've been looking all over for you. Where's your phone?" Bess called to me.

I dug into my purse and pulled out my phone. The battery had gone dead. Again. "I must have forgotten to charge it. Is everything okay?"

"We found Lexi. She's in bad shape," George said.

"Is she hurt?" I said, my voice spiking with nerves.

Bess shook her head. "Just shaken up. She received another note."

She handed me the black-smudged sky blue paper:

LAST WARNING: GET ON THAT FLOAT TOMORROW, AND YOU'LL BE SORRY.

"Ladies and gentlemen," Mr. Steele's voice boomed gruffly over the loudspeaker. "Please take your seats. The fireworks display is about to begin."

"Jeez," George said. "He sounds about as excited as a fourth-place Olympic finalist."

"I've been looking for Aly Stanfield everywhere," I told the girls. "Has anyone seen her?"

"Not me," said George.

Bess shook her head.

I rubbed at my temples with my fingers. I was not about to let Lexi's saboteur slip through my fingers before tomorrow afternoon's parade. After all the things that had gone wrong at the carnival today, who knew what this person was capable of doing next?

"So it wasn't Sunshine," Bess said. It wasn't a question.

"No," I said miserably. "It wasn't."

Suddenly a pair of arms wrapped me up from behind. All I could think of was the figure in the black hooded sweater. I gasped.

"Nancy!" Ned said, as I turned to face him. "Calm down, it's just me! I'm guessing things have gone from bad to worse since we last spoke?"

"You guessed correctly," I said. "Have you seen Aly Stanfield?" I crossed my fingers for an affirmative response.

"Actually, I just saw her. She and Lexi were setting

up a blanket on the front lawn to watch the fireworks. Which is what I hoped we could do . . ." He held up a soft gray blanket, grinning from ear to ear.

I felt awful. "Ned, I'm so sorry—but if I don't find Aly soon, I'm afraid she might do something drastic. She's hiding something big, and I have to find out what it is before it's too late."

Ned rubbed his hand comfortingly over my right shoulder. "You do what you need to do—I'll be right here waiting."

I grinned. Sometimes I wondered how I'd gotten so lucky with a guy like Ned.

"Do you want us to go with you?" Bess asked.

"No," I said, automatically. But then I thought back to how I'd felt inside the school. All alone, with no one to hear me if I yelled. And that had been just this afternoon. But I didn't want to worry anyone, so I said, "Actually, Bess, you can stay with Ned and watch the fireworks. But George, would you mind tagging along? Since my phone is dead, I won't be able to call you with any tech-related questions that might come up."

George smiled. "Of course!" she said.

We said our good-byes to Ned and Bess and headed back toward the fro-yo stand. Last time I'd gone by it, it had been shut down for the evening. But I guessed it was worth one last look. After that, the plan was to canvass the computer lab and look for clues there.

"Watch it!"

I looked down to find Heather Harris sitting on a blanket with what must have been her mother, father, and little brother.

"Sorry!" I said. I'd been trying to tiptoe through the maze of people who'd collected on the campus football field to watch the fireworks, but as it got more crowded, and my kitten heels dug deeper into the ground, I was having a more difficult time than I'd anticipated.

"Clumsy much?" Heather asked me, narrowing her pretty eyes. She tucked a strand of strawberry blond hair behind a delicate ear, rolling her eyes at my lack of coordination.

"Heather," her mother scolded. "Don't be rude. I'm sure it was an accident." She looked up at me. "You'll have to excuse my daughter. She's relearning her manners this week."

Heather's little brother began to giggle.

"Shut up, Kyle!" Heather snapped.

The smile disappeared from Kyle's mischievous-looking face.

"Heather," her mother repeated in a warning tone. "I've asked you not to use language like that. You have no right to address your brother that way. One more word from you, and you'll be spending another

two weeks without Internet and cable. You hear me?"

Heather's face drained of color, and George gripped my hand.

"I'm sorry," Mrs. Harris told us. "I hope you girls enjoy the fireworks."

"We—," I started, but my mind was whirling.

"We will!" George squeaked, and rushed me brusquely through the crowds.

When we were finally off the football field and back on the fairgrounds, George and I locked eyes.

"We need to think about this. Not . . . jump to any hasty conclusions. I mean, why would Heather Harris do this to her own best friend?" I asked. "At least Aly had a motive—her own mother passed her over for the DRH. What's Heather's excuse?"

"Harris?" George asked, her eyes growing in diameter.

"Heather Harris," I said. "That's Heather's last name. Why do you have that look on your face?"

"Every year," George spat out, "I go to this gaming convention in Chicago."

"Okay," I said.

"I won every single year for, like, four years straight. Then this kid comes along. This freckle-faced boy who couldn't have been older than twelve."

"Kyle Harris," I said, the realization dawning on me.

George nodded her head. "He won every year after

that. Well, except last year, when I kicked his little butt back into second place where it belongs." She smirked.

"George," I said, "focus. I think I know the answer to this, but would Kyle Harris have the ability to help his big sister block the IP of a certain blog so that people wouldn't be able to trace it?"

"Absolutely," George said with certainty.

"I need your phone," I told her hurriedly. The first gentle pop of a firework was going off in the distance, and it would only get louder as the display went forward.

"What for?" she asked.

"George! Your phone!"

"Okay, okay," she said, reluctantly pulling it out of her pocket. "No need to go all Heather Harris on me."

I gave her a warning look and then began dialing a number. I was trying to dial so fast, I messed it up three times before actually being able to press send.

"Hello? Who is this and why do you have my number?" Lexi squawked.

"Lexi, it's me. Nancy," I said. "Don't tell anyone you're talking to me, okay?" I added hastily.

"Uhhhhh, okay," she said. "Why did you call?"

"I just need to ask you one thing," I said.

"Shoot," said Lexi.

"That day you introduced yourself to me in Club Coffee . . . was there anyone there with you?"

"No," Lexi said. "Not that I remember."

My heart sank, and I kicked at the loose gravel beneath my obnoxious shoes.

"Oh wait!" Lexi chimed in. "That's not true—I was meeting Heather. She was there doing computer research for some school assignment. Her mom had just revoked her Internet privileges at home."

There was a pause while everything sunk in.

"Nan—I mean, hello?" Lexi asked. "Why does it matter who I was with?"

"Lexi," I said slowly. "The question I'm about to ask you is very important. You *have* to be honest with me if we're going to catch the person who's been harassing you."

"Anything," she said, her voice wobbling.

"Have you ever done anything to Heather that might make her feel angry with you?"

There was a pause, and another firework went off in the distance, louder this time—the brilliant sprays of light whistling as they cascaded down.

"Who told you that?" Lexi demanded, her voice strong and defiant.

"Told me what?" I asked. "I only asked if you'd ever—"

"I know what you asked," Lexi cut me off. She sounded murderous, and I could hear movement in the background.

130

"Lexi, please, just tell me what—"

"Aly Stanfield is dead," she said.

"Lexi, you have to stay calm and tell me what's going on," I soothed, trying to keep the panic out of my own voice.

But Lexi wasn't talking to me anymore. She was talking to herself, and I just happened to be on the other end of the line.

"She told Heather about Brad," Lexi seethed.

And then the line went dead.

BRAD33

"We'd better find Aly," I said to George. "What happened?" George asked, incredulous.

"My guess?" I said. "In those texts, it was clear that Aly was hiding something from one of her friends, and she didn't like it."

"So what does that have to do with Lexi?" asked George.

"I think that whatever the secret was had to do with Lexi and Brad. And if Aly were to spill, it would hurt her. When I asked if Heather had anything against her, Lexi freaked and said she wanted to kill Aly. So what if Aly did spill, and the person she spilled to was Heather?"

"We need to go back to Heather, stat," said George. "Agreed."

Getting back was even more difficult than getting out of the crowd. More people had gathered to see the fireworks display. It had also grown darker out, so the only chance I had to see anyone clearly was when the next burst of fireworks went off. I had nearly tripped over half a dozen people before we came upon Heather's scowling face.

"Mrs. Harris?" I asked.

She looked up at me, smiling.

"Would you mind if I stole your daughter for a moment? I have a school question I want to . . ." But she was already smiling and nodding her head. Her gaze was back on the fireworks display.

Now, I mouthed to Heather's obstinate expression.

She rolled her eyes and stood up, dusting nonexistent dirt from her pants. We led her behind the bleachers, which provided some small refuge from the noise of the fireworks.

"We need to talk," I told her.

She smirked, shaking her head slowly. "So Nancy Drew finally solves the big case." She giggled. "What did she promise you in return, best friends for life? Italian cashmere? Whatever it is, it's not worth it."

"But why?" I asked. "I thought you were Lexi's closest friend."

Heather crossed her arms over her chest and gazed up at the brilliant rainbows of lights in the sky. They lit up her delicate features, and when she looked back down at me, her eyes shimmered with tears.

"I thought so too," she said. "But apparently not. Aly found out a secret about Lexi. She tried to play it cool, but I've known Aly since third grade. She's a terrible liar."

"What was the secret?" asked George.

Heather looked back and forth between us. "She started seeing my boyfriend behind my back."

"Brad," I said. "Brad33."

Heather tossed a confused look toward me, then shrugged. "I was devastated. Brad and I had been dating for years. We were going to get *married* after college." She bit her lip. "I didn't say anything to Lexi—I promised Aly I wouldn't. But I couldn't just act as though nothing had happened."

"So you started the blog," I said.

"Yeah, I did. At first I wanted it to look like I was making fun of all of us. I thought it would be too obvious otherwise. But the more I hung out with Lexi, and the more she lied straight to my face, the more I wanted people to know about her. The fact that she was chosen as the DRH—and over *Aly*—that was the last straw."

"Is that why you started writing the notes?" I asked.

"What notes?"

George and I exchanged a look. "The notes on the blue paper?" I said.

"Ring any bells?" George asked.

"I don't have any idea what you're talking about," said Heather.

"Heather," I soothed. "I understand why you felt the need to do the blog. But the notes . . . those took things to a whole other level. The threats are really scaring Lexi. You've gotten your revenge on her, okay? It's time to come clean to her about the fact that you wrote those notes."

"Look," Heather said. "The blog was all me. I'll say that to her face. But I would never threaten her. I don't care if you believe me or not—those notes had nothing to do with me!" She tucked her hair behind her ears, regained her composure, and stood up straighter. "I've got to go find Aly."

And then she walked away.

Bess, George, and I were curled up on my bed, eating some of my housekeeper Hannah Gruen's famous oatmeal chocolate chip cookies.

"Is it down?" I asked George.

She turned her netbook to face me, stuffing another

cookie in her mouth. Where hatethesegirls.com had once been, now a page came up that said DOMAIN NAME NOT FOUND.

"Thanks, George," I said. "I get why she did it, but I still didn't feel right about keeping it up there."

Bess nodded. "You did the right thing, Nancy. No one deserves that."

"Even Lexi," George grumbled.

"So Heather didn't write those notes?" Bess asked with her mouth full.

"So she claims," said George skeptically.

"The truth is, none of us know the answer. I hate to say this, girls," I said, picking up my fifth cookie of the evening. "But . . ."

"We have another mystery on our hands," George and Bess chorused.

I giggled, nearly choking on my cookie crumbs. My friends knew me so well, and I wouldn't trade them for anyone else in the world.

It had been a long, exhausting day, and we all needed to get a good night's sleep and relax in front of the TV with one another—and Hannah's cookies, of course. It felt good to not be in heels. And it felt good to be surrounded by friends.

But I couldn't help it, my mind was already working on the next mystery. I loved my friends, and I wished I could just enjoy this moment—another mystery, solved. But I couldn't enjoy it, not really. Because the truth was, something was telling me that those notes, the figure, and the brick thrown through Aly Stanfield's window—even the sabotage of the carnival itself—might all be connected.

Whatever happened, we knew that it was all going to come to a climax at tomorrow's River Heights Celebration parade. I remembered the countdown to the parade on Heather's blog and wondered if there wasn't more to the story. Lexi and Heather had it out in the middle of the fireworks display. Though they were both equally to blame, I was certain that they'd never be able to patch things up.

Aly was left in the middle, with Lexi angry at her for telling Heather about her and Brad, and Heather angry at her for siding with Lexi. Secretly, I thought Aly's life would be a little bit better if she dumped them both and went back to being friends with Sunshine. But I knew that wasn't how high school worked. And there was no telling what would come of that.

There was still another mystery to solve. And it had to be done before tomorrow afternoon's parade.

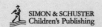